The Mum Mystery

Gwyneth Rees is half Welsh and half English and grew up in Scotland. She went to Glasgow University and qualified as a doctor in 1990. She is a child and adolescent psychiatrist but has now stopped practising so that she can write full-time. She is the author of *The Mum Hunt*, *The Mum Detective*, *My Mum's from Planet Pluto* and *The Making of May*, as well as the bestselling Fairies series and *Mermaid Magic* for younger readers. She lives in London with her two cats.

Visit www.gwynethrees.com

D0308769

Gwyneth Rees

The Mum Mystery

MACMILLAN CHILDREN'S BOOKS

First published 2007 by Macmillan Children's Books
a division of Macmillan Publishers Limited
20 New Wharf Road, London N1 9RR
Basingstoke and Oxford
www.panmacmillan.com

Associated companies throughout the world

ISBN 978-0-330-44212-1

3 5 7 9 8 6 4 2

A CIP catalogue record for this book is available from
the British Library.

Typeset by Intype Libra Ltd
Printed and bound in Great Britain by Mackays of Chatham plc, Kent

For Rosie and Hannah Duthie

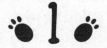

Most of what I'm about to tell you would never have happened if Nevada Moriarty hadn't moved into our street, so I guess I should start with the day I first found out she was here. It was a Wednesday afternoon in mid-November – the same Wednesday that my big brother, Matthew, decided to play truant from school. (Matthew is sixteen – four years older than me – and it isn't like him to skip school. For one thing he's always too worried about his next lot of exams to want to miss too many lessons, and for another he knows he'll really get it from our dad if he gets caught.)

I would never have known that my brother had skipped school if it wasn't for Holly. Holly is not only my best friend (and has been since we were little), she's Matthew's greatest admirer. She's fancied him for ages, even though he's never had any time for her. Holly's interest in my brother includes memorizing his entire school timetable, so she knows what days he has PE. His class were doing cross-country running every Wednesday afternoon that term, which meant that if you happened to be looking out of one of the upstairs classroom windows at the right time, you could spot him and his classmates jogging three times round the grassy perimeter of the playing fields.

'He's not there and neither is Jake,' Holly informed me as we stood at the bench by the window in the science lab, trying to turn different solids into liquids with the help of a Bunsen burner. She had taken off her protective goggles in order to see out of the window better, and now our science teacher noticed and started yelling at her to put them back on again.

Jake is my brother's best friend, and if both of them were missing then I guessed they must be playing truant together. They'd certainly both been at school earlier, because I'd seen them in the school canteen at lunchtime.

Before I could respond, our deputy head, Miss Dumont, came into the room to speak to our teacher. Nobody likes Miss Dumont because she's very strict and she speaks in a dead snooty voice and she doesn't ever joke with us like most of our other teachers do.

'I wonder what *she* wants,' I murmured.

'Maybe she's found out about Matthew bunking off and she's come to ask you if you know where he is,' Holly said.

But it turned out that our deputy head was there for a totally different reason. She had come to announce that a new girl, whose name was Nevada, would be starting in our class the following day.

A few people started to giggle and the name *Nevada* got repeated all around the room, accompanied by sniggers.

Miss Dumont glared at us and added sternly, 'I expect you *all* to make her feel welcome. Is that clear?'

Then she called out my name – my full first name, which I really don't appreciate being called in public. 'Esmerelda Harvey, I believe you and Nevada live in the same street, so I want you to make a special effort to look after her while she gets to know everybody.'

Everyone stared at me then, including Holly. Billy Sanderson, who is always trying to wind me up, grinned at me from across the room, and I reckoned he might be planning on calling me Esmerelda all the time from now on.

'You never said you had new neighbours,' Holly whispered when Miss Dumont had gone and our science teacher had told us to start clearing up because it was nearly the end of the period.

'I didn't know we did,' I whispered back as I unplugged our Bunsen burner from the gas tap. I was puzzled, because generally I tend to know about most of the things that are going on in our street.

'Well, wait and see what she's like before you get too friendly with her,' Holly warned me.

I nodded. 'Holly, listen,' I said. 'I'm wondering if Matthew's skipping school because he's so upset about Jennifer dumping him.' (Jennifer had been my brother's girlfriend for the last three months, and when she'd told him that she wanted to end things a few days earlier, Matthew had been devastated.)

'I don't see why. Matthew's well rid of her, if you ask me!'

'Yeah, well I don't think *he* sees it that way,' I told her. 'He's pretty cut up about it.'

'That's because he's sensitive,' she replied matter-of-factly. 'So am I, so I know how he feels. Jennifer wasn't sensitive, you see, which is why they weren't at all suited.'

'Well, I still think we should try and find a way of getting them back together,' I said firmly. 'Matty's really miserable without her.' My brother had been shut up in his room playing depressing music ever since Jennifer had dumped him, and every mealtime he'd just picked at his food and hardly eaten a thing.

'No way,' Holly said. 'I already told you. Jennifer isn't right for him.'

'You're only saying that because *you* fancy him,' I protested.

'No I'm not!'

I sighed impatiently, because I've never been able to understand this stupid crush my friend has on my brother. 'I don't know why you fancy him anyway, Holly. He's always swearing and farting and stuff – and he's got a really spotty back.' I could have added that since she was the same age as me she didn't stand a chance anyhow, but I didn't want to be that cruel.

Holly shook her head as if she didn't believe me. 'You're just trying to put me off. I mean, why are you so keen to get Jennifer to take him back if he's that gross?'

'Jennifer's not my best friend,' I pointed out. '*You* are.'

'I don't care. I'm still not helping you get them back together,' Holly said stubbornly.

'I guess I'll just have to do something about it on my own then, won't I?' I told her.

'I don't see why. I mean, Matthew hasn't *asked* for your help, has he?'

'*So?*' I answered impatiently.

Holly knows as well as I do that nobody in my family has ever actually *asked* for my help. And she also knows that I've never let that stop me before.

When I got home from school my brother was already there, and for once he wasn't in his room playing miserable music. He was in the kitchen with Jake. They had the door closed and they were talking inside in low voices, so I crept up close and put one ear against the door to listen. (You'd think my brother would know by now that it isn't safe to speak about secret things when I'm anywhere nearby – but he never seems to learn.)

'Come on, Matt, it'll be a laugh,' Jake was saying.

'Not if we get caught,' Matthew replied.

'We won't get caught. No one'll see us. Look, you can't back out now – not when we've just bought the stuff.' Jake paused for a moment before adding, 'Anyway, I reckon this'll really take your mind off Jennifer.'

'I'm *over* Jennifer,' Matthew said sharply, but I thought I heard his voice tremble a bit. 'Look, if we do this, we've got to make sure nobody knows it's us. You know what my dad's like. If he thinks I've—'

At that moment my foot accidentally pushed

the door, making it creak, so I had no choice but to walk into the room.

My brother glared at me. 'What do *you* want?'

'I know you and Jake skipped school this afternoon,' I told him. 'You're going to get into trouble if Dad finds out.'

'Yeah, well he won't find out, will he? Not unless some nosy interfering little person tells him.'

'I am *not* nosy and interfering!' I retorted indignantly.

'Yeah, *right*.'

I ignored that and demanded, 'So where were you?'

But he tapped his nose and turned away and I knew I wasn't going to get any more information out of him.

We were the only ones in the house. Dad never usually gets back from work until at least seven o'clock. He's a police detective and he sometimes has to work even later than that. We don't have a mum, and Dad's girlfriend didn't seem to be here either.

'Where's Lizzie?' I asked.

Wednesday is Lizzie's half-day and she'd said she'd be here when I got home from school this afternoon. She was cooking for us tonight, which is always a bit of a hit-and-miss affair. (Lasagne and chilli con carne were the only two dishes she knew how to cook when she first met us, and since then her efforts to try out new recipes haven't always gone according to plan.)

Matthew handed me a note Lizzie had left on the table. It said she had gone to show her flat to someone who might want to rent it from her.

'Oh great!' I said enthusiastically. 'Maybe Lizzie'll get her flat rented out today and then she'll be able to come and live with us straight away!' (Lizzie and Dad had been together for a whole year now and she had recently agreed to move in with us.)

Matty looked sour-faced as he replied, 'Don't expect Lizzie to definitely move in, Esmie. It's a well-known fact that women are totally unreliable.'

'Lizzie isn't unreliable!' I burst out indignantly. I thought Lizzie was wonderful, and ever since Dad had met her, I'd thought she'd make the perfect stepmum.

'Well just don't count on her moving in for good,' my brother grunted.

'Hey, ease off, Matt,' Jake said, seeing how upset I was looking.

'Well, Esmie should face the truth. I mean,

why do *you* think she wants to rent out her flat rather than sell it?' he asked me.

I just looked at him dumbly, feeling my lower lip trembling.

'Because she wants to have somewhere to move back to, if she gets fed up with living with *us*,' he finished bitterly.

I stared at my brother, tears welling up in my eyes.

'Ignore him, Esmie,' Jake said, giving Matthew a sharp nudge in the ribs. 'He's just got it in for the opposite sex at the moment, because of Jennifer. Isn't that right, mate?'

Matthew just shrugged. He wasn't even looking guilty, which he usually does if he manages to make me cry.

Suddenly I felt really angry.

'Did Dad *say* you could have Jake round after school?' I snapped. 'Cos you know you're not allowed to hang out with your mates until you've done your homework.'

'Get lost, Esmie,' Matthew muttered.

'No – Esmie's got a point,' Jake said quickly. 'We'd better leave now, in case your dad comes home early or something. We don't want him having one of his hairy fits and grounding you.' He grinned. 'God, your dad is *sooo* strict.'

'Tell me about it,' Matthew said grumpily. 'I wish my dad was more like yours.' (Jake's dad is really cool and prides himself on being more of a friend to Jake than anything else. But when Matty once suggested to Dad that the two of *them* might get on better if Dad acted more like a mate to *him*, Dad had just laughed. 'You've got enough mates, Matthew – you don't need another. What you *need* is a parent – and I'm only sorry you haven't got more of those.' That was Dad's way of saying he was sorry that we didn't have a mother as well as a father – our mum died when I was born, so he's had to bring us up pretty much on his own.)

'So are you coming or what?' Jake said, heading for the door.

'I'll come round to yours as soon as Lizzie gets back,' Matthew replied. He's not allowed to leave me in the house by myself and he only ever does it if he can bribe me not to tell Dad.

'*Then* we'll go and do it, right?' Jake said.

Matthew nodded. 'Right.'

'Go and do *what*?' I asked.

But Matty just tapped his nose and wouldn't tell me a thing.

• 2 •

As soon as Lizzie arrived home at a quarter to six, Matthew announced that he was going out.

Lizzie immediately looked uncertain about whether or not that was OK. 'What about your homework?' she asked him. 'You can't have finished it yet, can you?' (Now that Matty's in the senior part of the school he always gets loads of homework and it always takes him at least until dinner-time to get it done.)

'I'll finish it later,' Matty said.

'Well . . .' Lizzie looked like she was floundering. She's pretty confident about standing in for Dad where I'm concerned, but when it's something involving Matty, I've noticed she's always a lot less certain.

'See you!' Matty said abruptly, and he was through the front door before Lizzie could say anything else.

I had more important things on my mind

however. 'Did that person want to rent out your flat, Lizzie?' I asked her eagerly.

She shook her head. 'But there's someone else coming to have a look at it tomorrow.'

'Oh good,' I said, beaming at her.

By the time Dad arrived home, Lizzie had made a shepherd's pie (her first one ever) and she was so thrilled by the fact that it wasn't burnt on the top that she had forgotten all about my brother. It was only when Dad asked me to go and tell Matthew that dinner was ready that we remembered he wasn't in.

We held back dinner for a while and finally, after Dad had left two grumpy messages on my brother's mobile, we sat down at the kitchen table without him.

'I hope he's all right,' Lizzie said as she served out the food. 'You know, he really hasn't been himself since Jennifer broke up with him.'

That's when we heard the front door open.

'MATTHEW!' Dad yelled, and when my brother didn't appear, he got up from the table and went out to the hall.

I quickly followed him, pretending not to hear Lizzie telling me to stay put.

Matty was on his way up the stairs, still wearing his outdoor jacket.

'Where do you think you're going?' Dad barked at him.

My brother stopped in his tracks and turned round. I should probably mention now that I want to be a detective when I grow up (though I haven't decided yet whether I want to be a *police* detective like Dad, or a *private* detective like Sherlock Holmes) and that I like to practise my detecting skills whenever possible. And since detectives can often get clues from a person's appearance after they've committed a crime, I was now studying my brother's hair, face and clothes very carefully. There didn't seem to be anything unusual about him, apart from the fact that he had a very guilty look on his face – but that might have just been because he knew he was late home for dinner.

'I thought I'd just go and have a quick shower,' Matty muttered.

'You'll come and eat with us right now!' Dad snapped.

'Matty, it's shepherd's pie and it's really nice,' I put in cheerily.

'Esmie, go and sit down,' Dad said.

I did as I was told and Dad followed me, so we were both sitting down again at the table by the time Matty entered the kitchen. He had taken off his outdoor jacket and it was only now that we saw he was limping slightly.

'Are you all right, Matthew?' Lizzie asked in a concerned voice.

'Yeah,' he grunted, sitting down very gingerly and wincing as he made contact with the seat.

'Matthew, what's wrong with you?' Dad said impatiently.

'Nothing. I fell over and got a graze, that's all.'

Lizzie had served out some shepherd's pie on to my brother's plate and he picked up his fork and began to pick at it.

'So where did you and Jake go?' I asked curiously.

'Nowhere,' my brother replied, giving me a *back off* sort of look.

'Actually, Matthew, I was just going to ask the same thing,' Dad said sternly.

'We were just hanging out, that's all.'

'And what about your homework? Lizzie says you left the house at six o'clock.'

'Yeah . . . sorry . . .' Matty looked agitated, and put down his fork with the food still on it. (Hercule, our black and white kitten, came padding across the kitchen at that point, and positioned himself under my brother's chair, clearly having high hopes for the quality of tonight's leftovers.)

And that's when I decided to help my brother out. Don't ask me why.

'Guess what?' I said, before Dad could do any more interrogating. 'There's a new girl starting in my class tomorrow and Miss Dumont says she lives in our street. But we haven't had any new neighbours move into our street recently, have we, Dad?'

Dad looked at me. 'Mrs Lewis was telling me that Frank and Ruth across the road have got their nieces moving in with them – two girls the same ages as you and Matty apparently.'

'Really?' I immediately felt excited.

'Yes. Of course, Mrs Lewis isn't very happy about it.'

'Why not?' I asked.

'She says she thinks there are enough children in this street as it is.' (Mrs Lewis is our next-door neighbour. She's very old and very cranky and it's a family joke that she'd be perfect as the child-eating witch in *Hansel and Gretel*.)

'Charming,' Lizzie said, smiling.

'I know. I reckon she still hasn't forgiven Frank and Ruth for the geranium incident.' (Last summer Mr Stevens – that's Frank – had complained to Mrs Lewis that her cat, Pixie, had been peeing on his geraniums. Needless to say, Mrs Lewis had been furious. 'Who does he think he is, to talk like that about my Pixie?' she had ranted. '*All* geraniums smell like cat wee – and that's what I told him.')

'Nevada must be *their* niece then,' I said. 'Holly and I think she might be American or something because of her name.'

Just then the phone started ringing and Matthew pushed back his chair. (He had left loads of messages on Jennifer's phone since she'd dumped him, and every time our phone rang he always looked full of hope that it would be her.)

'Stay there,' Dad told him, getting up. 'If it's for you, you can ring back after dinner.'

'If it's Jennifer, Matty had better speak to her straight away, Dad,' I pointed out. 'Otherwise she might think he's deliberately playing it cool.'

'Yes, well that might not be such a bad thing,' Dad replied as he left the room.

'Gee – thanks, Dad!' my brother exploded.

Lizzie quickly put her hand on his forearm. 'Matty, all your dad means is that maybe you *should* play it a bit cooler with Jennifer.'

'Yeah, well maybe I can't afford to, OK?' Matty retorted, and his eyes started to fill with tears. 'Maybe she just doesn't like me that much!'

'Sweetheart, if that's true then you're better

off without her,' Lizzie said, giving his arm a squeeze. 'Believe me, there are lots of other girls out there who'd love to have you as a boyfriend.'

Matthew sniffed and didn't say anything.

I kept quiet, kind of mesmerized, because seeing Lizzie acting all soft and motherly like that was really nice. Then Dad came back into the room and Lizzie moved her hand away from Matty's arm. (She's a bit self-conscious about showing her feelings for us in front of Dad, I've noticed.)

'That was Jake's mother,' Dad said, frowning at my brother. 'She says the two of you skipped school today. She says a friend of hers saw you in a paint shop in town. Is that true?'

My detective's ears pricked up at that. Could this have something to do with the secret thing that Matty and Jake had been plotting earlier?

Matty looked nervous. 'We were just hanging out, Dad. We weren't doing anything wrong.'

'Oh, so playing truant from school isn't wrong then?'

'We only missed PE.'

'That's not the point. The point is, when you tell me you're in school, that's where I expect you to be.'

'I know, Dad. I'm sorry.' Matthew pushed

his plate away, looking miserable. 'Can I leave the table please?' His food was completely uneaten.

Dad nodded. 'Go and do your homework. I'll come and speak to you later.'

And as Matthew limped out of the kitchen, I noticed that the seat of his jeans was torn slightly and that there was something on the material that looked suspiciously like blood.

3

When I arrived at school the next day there was a big crowd standing at the school gate and straight away I saw that they were all laughing and pointing up at our school sign.

'Hello, Esmie,' a voice said as I tried to get near enough to see what everyone was looking at. I turned to see Mrs Stevens, who lives in the house across the road. There was a girl my own age standing beside her. 'This is my niece, Nevada,' she said. 'Nevada, this is Esmie.'

'Hi,' the girl mumbled.

'Hi,' I said, staring at her. She was wearing a bright green coat that made her stand out in a way I wouldn't have wanted to if I'd just been starting at a new school. Otherwise she looked quite ordinary. She was a bit smaller than me and slim, with long dark hair and dark eyes, which weren't looking at me but were fixed, along with everyone else's, on the school sign.

Under the name of our school, the sign's red lettering now said:

Head teacher: Mr Thick
Deputy head teacher: Miss Dumb

Someone had done a brilliant job of spray-painting over the end letters and changing the 'a' and 'o' of Mr Thackery and Miss Dumont's names. They'd obviously taken a tumble while they were doing it though, because the section of wooden fence beside the gate (which you'd have to stand on to reach the sign) had collapsed and was lying in splintery sections on the ground.

That's when I noticed my brother and Jake standing further back from everybody else, grinning and whispering to each other. I stared at them. Was it possible that this was the secret thing they'd been plotting? It wasn't really like Matty to do something this bold – but then he had been in a really strange mood lately. And if they had done this it would explain why they had skipped school yesterday and gone to a paint shop.

The school bell rang and everyone started moving away, including Nevada and her aunt.

As soon as I got to my first class of the day – which was French – I told Holly my suspicions about my brother. I'm allowed to sit next to Holly in French, though in a lot of other classes I'm not, because the teachers reckon the two of us talk too much. Everyone in our class was discussing what had happened to the school sign, and Miss Murphy was late coming to the lesson, so I reckoned all the teachers must be gossiping about the same thing in the staffroom. I just hoped that Matthew and Jake didn't get caught. Of course I didn't have any proof that it was them, but I reckoned all the facts were pointing to it.

'Matthew is *so* cool,' Holly whispered to me after I'd told her.

'Yes, but you mustn't tell anyone it was him, Holly,' I whispered back.

'Of course not! Do you think I'm stupid?'

'No, it's just . . .' I trailed off, not wanting to make her cross with me. It's just that Holly wants to be a journalist when she grows up – a Gossip Columnist to be precise – and she tends to do a lot of practising whenever she can. Don't get me wrong – Holly's a really loyal friend and I know if I specifically *tell* her to keep quiet about something then she will. It's just that sometimes I've mentioned things that I've just *assumed* she won't repeat to anyone else and I've found out by the end of the day that the whole class knows. And if I get annoyed about it she just says it's my own fault for not making it clear that what I'd told her was confidential.

We were working in pairs twenty minutes later, taking it in turns to be a French shop-keeper and a customer, when there was a knock on the door and Miss Dumont walked in. There were a few giggles, but Miss Dumont ignored them. She didn't look any more annoyed than usual – but then her face always looks pretty cross in any case.

Nevada was with her. (In all the fuss about the sign I'd forgotten to tell Holly that I'd already met her at the school gate and that her accent definitely wasn't American.)

There were a few smiles but no sniggers when Miss Dumont introduced her to the class, though I saw Billy Sanderson grinning at me from the other side of the room, mouthing, 'Esmerelda.'

Nevada was holding her coat over her arm, and apart from her tie she was wearing what I guessed must be the uniform of her old school. Her skirt and cardigan were grey whereas ours were navy. She was looking nervous as we all stared at her.

Miss Murphy sorted out a seat for her and I saw Miss Dumont glance in my direction as she said something to our French teacher in a low voice, but it wasn't until later, after the bell had gone and we were all leaving the room to go to the next class, that Miss Murphy called me over to her desk.

'Esmie, Miss Dumont says that you've agreed to look after Nevada until she settles in. Could you wait for a moment while I have a quick word with her? Then you can take her to your next lesson.'

Nevada was looking at me and I gave her what I hoped was a reassuring smile. Luckily I've never had to change schools myself – apart from moving up to secondary school with everybody else – but I reckon it must be pretty nerve-racking.

'Esmie'll be late for maths if she waits, miss,' Holly spoke up from the doorway, where she was standing holding my school bag for me.

Miss Murphy obviously felt a bit irritated with Holly's bossiness, because she said quite briskly, 'Holly, I'd like you to go and tell your maths teacher that Esmie and Nevada will be following in five minutes.'

'Yes, but—' my friend started to argue, but Miss Murphy cut her short.

'Thank you, Holly.'

And Holly had no choice but to do as she was told.

*

I knew as soon as I'd spent a few minutes alone with Nevada that she wasn't as ordinary as I'd first thought. For starters she had a really intense way of looking at you, as if she could tell exactly what you were thinking.

'Sorry if I've got you in trouble with your friend,' she said as we walked along the corridor towards our maths class.

'Don't be daft,' I replied, though I knew Holly *would* be in a bad mood when I met up with her in maths. (She's a bit possessive in case you haven't guessed – and she *really* doesn't like being left out of things.) 'I guess we're neighbours, since my house is just across the road from yours,' I added.

She nodded. 'Aunt Ruth told me.'

'Are you staying here for a while then?'

'A few months probably. My dad has to travel a lot with his work and he's had to go to Saudi Arabia. Mum's gone with him but she thought it was best if Carys and I stayed with our aunt and uncle, so we could go to school here. They might buy a house here after they come back – if Dad doesn't have to move to the opposite end of the country or something.'

'Carys is your sister, right?'

She nodded. 'She's just said that she wants to quit school and get a job instead. Aunt Ruth and her were arguing about it at breakfast this morning. She's sixteen, so it's legal for her to quit school, but my parents want her to stay on and do A levels.'

'My dad and my big brother are always having massive rows,' I told her. 'It's a real pain, isn't it?'

'Yeah – when my dad finds out about Carys, he's going to hit the roof.'

'So what does your dad do?' I asked her. (I always like asking people what their fathers do, because then I get to tell them that mine is a police detective, which I reckon is just about the coolest job there is.)

'He's an engineer for an oil company. He gets to travel all over the place and usually we have to go with him. Mum can do her job any-where, so it doesn't matter to her. She's a psychic,' she added proudly.

'*Really?*' Suddenly, having a detective for a dad didn't seem quite as exciting as it usually did.

'Yes, but she doesn't like me to talk about it too much.' She lowered her voice. 'For confidentiality reasons.'

'Wow!' I quickly recovered enough to add, 'That sounds just like my dad. He's a police detective and he can't talk about *his* work for confidentiality reasons either.'

'Oh . . .' Nevada sounded surprised, as if she hadn't expected my dad to have a job that was even the slightest bit as cool as her mum's. 'The thing is,' she continued, 'I'm going to be a psychic too, when I grow up. That sort of thing runs in families, you see.'

'That's just how it is with me,' I gushed. 'I want to be a detective like my dad.'

Nevada was looking interested now. 'You know, I think it would be really cool to be the sort of psychic who helps detectives with their investigations – the kind who helps find missing people and where dead bodies have been hidden and stuff like that.'

'Wow!' I gasped. 'That *would* be cool!'

Unfortunately we couldn't continue our conversation because we'd arrived outside our maths classroom. But there was just time for Nevada to ask, 'Can I walk home from school with you today?' and for me to nod enthusiastically in reply.

After maths it was break-time, and our teacher wanted to talk to Nevada, so I went with Holly to the canteen, where we're allowed to hang out if we don't want to go outside. Holly was bursting with questions, so I told her some of what Nevada had told me – that her mum was a psychic and that she wanted to be one too when she grew up.

Holly started to laugh. 'You mean her mum's like one of those gypsies at the fair – the kind who sits and reads a crystal ball if you cross her palm with silver?'

'She never said she was a gypsy – but even if she is, so what?' I said hotly.

'Nothing – but I mean, would *you* want to have a mum who tells fortunes for a living? I bet she makes them all up!'

'You don't know that's what she does!' I retorted. 'Anyway, *I* think Nevada seems really nice.'

'Yeah, well you always think *everyone* is really nice. You thought that about Jennifer too, remember, and look how she's treated Matthew.'

'OK, so I did like Jennifer a lot more in the beginning,' I admitted, 'but I still don't think she's all that terrible. Anyway it's what Matthew thinks of her that counts, and he's really upset about them splitting up.'

Holly pulled a face and went off to talk to some other people in our class.

I sat down at one of the tables and started chatting to some girls I'm friendly with in the year above us. They were talking about how one of them had seen our school caretaker remove the school sign and carry it into the building just before break-time. They also seemed to think that no one had a clue who had done it, which I was relieved to hear. I hadn't seen Matthew or Jake since we'd been at the school gate this morning, and I hoped they were keeping a low profile.

'Hiya,' Holly said, coming back to join me. 'I just spoke to some of the others and *they* all think that having a mum who's a psychic is really weird too.'

'*Who's* got a mum who's a psychic?' one of our groups asked.

'The new girl in our class,' Holly replied. 'She's called Nevada.'

'*Nevada?*'

'I know.' Holly giggled. 'It's a seriously wacko name, isn't it?'

'Maybe all psychics give their kids weird names,' somebody joked.

Suddenly I saw that Nevada had found her way to the canteen and was walking towards us.

'Here she is,' I hissed. 'Just shut up, Holly, OK?'

'Don't tell *me* to shut up!'

I quickly jumped up and went to head off Nevada before she could reach our table. 'Come on,' I told her. 'It's really crowded in here. Let's go outside.'

I glanced back at Holly, who was looking at me as if *I* was the one who was doing something wrong. I couldn't understand why she was behaving like this. She's been my best friend since infant school and OK, so she's always been a bit possessive, but it wasn't as if I was ditching her for Nevada, was it?

As we made for the door, Billy Sanderson came towards us, grinning from ear to ear. He had a teacup in one hand, which he was waving about in front of him. 'Hey, Nevada, do you think your mum might give me a free tea-leaf reading? I mean, does she read tea leaves as well as crystal balls?'

All the kids nearby started to laugh, and Nevada's face went bright red. She looked at me accusingly. 'I should've known you'd think it was a joke,' she said.

'I didn't!' I exclaimed. 'I mean, I *don't*. Look, I didn't tell everyone, honestly. I just –'

But she had shoved Billy Sanderson's teacup out of the way and stalked off before I could finish protesting that the only person I had told was Holly, and that she was the one who had told everyone else – not me.

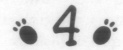

Needless to say Nevada didn't walk home with me after school, and when I tried to talk to Holly about what had happened she just shrugged and said Nevada was too sensitive.

I couldn't wait to tell Lizzie about it, because she's much more understanding than Dad when it comes to this sort of problem. (Dad tends to only listen for about two minutes to any worries I have concerning my friends, then he always interrupts with some completely inappropriate solution that's way too straight-forward and shows that he doesn't understand how complicated the situation is at all.)

When I got home Dad was there. Apparently some meeting he was meant to be attending had been cancelled at the last minute, and he'd decided to come home early. And he told me that Lizzie wasn't coming over that night because she had gone to see a friend.

I went upstairs to use the bathroom, and

when I came down again, Dad was in the kitchen loading the washing machine and Matthew was sitting at the table eating a cheese sandwich, telling Dad about some science experiment he'd done at school that had gone disastrously wrong.

'Hi, Matty,' I said, giving him a knowing look. It was the first chance I'd had to speak to him since leaving the house that morning.

'Whatevuh,' he grunted.

Dad was peering closely at a pair of Matty's jeans that he'd been about to put in the washing machine. They were the same ones my brother had been wearing the previous night and Dad had just noticed the tear in the seat of them. 'How did this happen, Matthew?' he asked.

'Dunno,' my brother grunted, not looking at him.

'It's *don't* know – and how can you not know?' Dad inspected the hole more closely. 'Is this blood?'

Matty was sitting on one butt cheek only, and Dad suddenly seemed to notice that. 'You couldn't sit down properly yesterday either. What's wrong with you?'

'I've got a bruise,' Matty grunted. 'I already told you – I fell, that's all. It's no big deal.'

'Yesterday you said it was a graze,' I pointed

out, which made my brother glare at me. (I don't know why, since I was only trying to help him keep his story straight.)

Dad was looking at the torn jeans again. 'You fell on *what* exactly?'

'Look – quit interrogating me, Dad! You're not at work now, OK?' Matty eased himself up off his chair and limped out of the room.

Dad sighed and bundled the jeans into the machine, looking like he was too tired to continue his investigation any further. I wasn't though, and I was about to follow my brother and find out more, when Dad said, 'I've got something to give you, Esmie.'

He left the washing and led me into the living room, where a large wooden box was sitting on the coffee table. 'I've been having a clear-out. I found your mother's old jewellery box up in the loft and I thought you might like it. It was given to her when she was your age, I think.'

The box was made of light-coloured wood with little flowers carved on the lid. It had a keyhole but no key. I opened it up. The hinges were pretty stiff.

'We can put a bit of oil on those if you like,' Dad said.

There was a tray inside that pulled out. Both the tray and the floor of the box were lined with thin red material that must have once looked quite plush, and both layers were separated into little sections that allowed you to organize your jewellery properly.

'So what do you think?' Dad asked.

'I love it!' I replied. 'Especially as it's my mother's. And if she got it when she was *my* age then it must be really old. Maybe it's an antique!'

Dad chuckled. 'Have a heart, Esmie. It wasn't that long ago.'

I picked up the box and told Dad I was going to take it into the kitchen to give it a polish before putting it up in my room.

I was still in the kitchen when the doorbell rang ten minutes later.

Dad went to answer it and I heard him say, 'Oh, hello, Jake.'

'How's it going, Mr Harvey?'

'Very well, thank you. How's it going for you?'

'Cool, thanks. Is Matt here?'

'He's upstairs doing his homework.'

'Is it OK if I go and talk to him quickly about something?'

'All right, but don't disturb him for too long.'

I was pretty sure I knew what the 'something' was about, so I waited for Dad to go back into the living room before sneaking upstairs after Jake.

I stood outside my brother's bedroom door and listened. I'm not supposed to do that but I *am* in training to be a detective and I reckon every detective has to break the rules sometimes to uncover the evidence.

'That's gross! You've got to do something about it!' Jake was exclaiming.

'I've tried,' Matty said. 'The top bit broke off when I tried to pull it out and now it's stuck.'

'Well, it'll have to come out. It looks pretty inflamed already.'

'What's going on?' I asked, pushing open the door.

'Esmie – *get out!*' Matty yelled, pulling up his trousers.

'What's wrong with you?' I demanded.

'He's got a massive splinter of wood stuck in his bum, that's what's wrong with him,' Jake said. 'I reckon you're gonna have to go to the doctor's to get it out, mate.'

'No way!'

'Is it a bit of wood from the school fence?' I asked.

'Shut up, Esmie!'

'I know it was you two who did the school sign,' I persisted. '*And* you broke the fence. That's vandalism, in case you didn't know!'

'Breaking the fence was an accident,' Jake said. 'Anyway, they can easily get it repaired.'

'Jake, shut up!' Matty snapped. 'Don't tell her anything, OK?' And he pushed me out through the door so hard that I nearly lost my balance.

'It'll serve you right if you have to get that splinter *cut* out,' I shouted to him. And I was so angry that I went into Dad's room and got straight on the phone to Holly.

As I'd expected, Holly was super-interested in what I had to tell her. She's always been more interested than most people in Matthew's bum, ever since she decided it was just like Brad Pitt's. (Don't ask me why Holly is so keen on Brad Pitt when there are loads of other actors who are much less ancient, but there you go.) However, instead of focusing on how obnoxious my brother had been to me, and how much trouble he was going to be in if our dad found out what he'd done, Holly seemed more worried that Matty was in grave danger of dying from his splinter. Before I knew it, she was talking about blood poisoning, gangrene and tetanus and saying that Matty had to go and see the doctor immediately. 'If he won't agree to go then you'll have to *make* him,' she said firmly.

'I can't make him,' I protested.

'Esmie, his life could be at stake!' Holly retorted. 'You have to act *now*.'

'But he won't listen to me.'

'No, but he'll have to listen if you tell your dad.'

'Holly, I can't,' I said. Holly is an only child so she doesn't know what a big deal it is to tell on your brother or sister – especially if you've got a dad like ours. Dad can't stand vandalism and he's also pretty intolerant when it comes to any misbehaving or mucking around Matthew or I might do in school.

'Yeah, well don't blame me if he ends up having to have half his bum amputated because you didn't act quickly enough,' Holly said stroppily.

By six o'clock that evening Matty was avoiding sitting down whenever possible and it was obviously very painful for him when he did.

'Have they brought back the cane in your school without me knowing?' Dad asked him as he watched Matty perch on the edge of his seat in order to eat his dinner. (We were having cheesy baked potatoes and ham salad.)

'Huh?'

'You're sitting like I used to after our headmaster gave me six of the best.' (Dad went to a very strict boys' school, which he didn't like much, but which he always likes to mention whenever we complain about *our* school being too hard on us.)

'Ha ha,' Matthew said drily.

'So why are you sitting like that?'

'I told you. I fell.'

I couldn't contain myself any longer. 'Tell him, Matty.'

Matthew glared at me as Dad looked at him and asked, 'Tell me what?'

'Nothing,' Matty snapped.

'He's got a big splinter of wood stuck in his bum, and Holly and I are worried he'll get gangrene or something if it doesn't get taken out,' I blurted.

Matty looked like he was about to strangle me.

Dad looked concerned. 'Is that true?'

'Yes, but it's no big deal,' my brother grunted.

'Holly reckons he might get tetanus as well,' I added.

Dad frowned. 'So how did this happen?'

'He was climbing over a fence,' I said, and I got glared at even more, despite the fact that I didn't say *which* fence. Then it occurred to me that climbing over fences was the sort of thing that burglars did and that Dad might jump to the wrong conclusion if I wasn't careful. 'He wasn't climbing into anyone's private property or anything though, were you, Matty?'

'Shut up, Esmie.' Matthew looked like he now thought death by strangulation was too good for me.

'Well, that's all very interesting, thank you, Esmie,' Dad said, turning back to fix his gaze firmly on my brother. 'So do you think I should take a look?'

'No,' Matty growled.

'Jake was really worried when *he* saw it,' I put in. '*He* thought Matty needed to see a doctor.'

'Esmie, just shut it, OK?'

'I expect he's shy because it's in his bottom.'

'SHUT UP, ESMIE!' Matty yelled.

'OK, that's enough,' Dad said. He was standing up and motioning for my brother to do the same. 'Come on. Let's go upstairs. I want to see how bad it is.'

'*No*, Dad!'

'Well if you don't want me to look, I'll make an appointment for you to see the doctor.'

'No way!'

'I expect he's embarrassed in case it's Doctor Gregg,' I said. Dr Gregg is the lady doctor in our practice. She's young and very pretty and my brother blushes every time he sees her –

and normally he only has to talk to her about his acne. 'Don't worry, Matty,' I added. 'She's a doctor, so she'll have seen *loads* of bums before yours.'

And that's when my brother picked up his baked potato and hurled it at me.

Dad went mad then. Matty got told off for throwing his food and I got told off for stirring things up, and we both got told to finish our dinners (minus the potato in Matthew's case) while Dad called the surgery to make an appointment for the following morning.

'Don't worry,' I whispered in a conciliatory way while Dad was on the phone in the living room. 'I won't tell him you fell on the school fence while you were painting the sign.'

But Matthew still seemed furious with me. 'Quit sticking your nose in where it doesn't belong, Esmie,' he snarled. 'I know you think you're Miss Marple or something, but if you ask me you'd make a really *rubbish* detective!'

And if my own baked potato hadn't been almost finished by then, I'd have thrown it at him for sure.

After dinner I went upstairs to use the bathroom and while I was in there I spotted a tiny fragment of grey wood on the side of the bath.

Grey is the colour of our school fence and I remembered how Matty had told Jake that he'd tried to dislodge the splinter himself, but that the top part had broken off. And since this was the closest thing to crime-scene evidence that I had encountered in a while, I rushed off to fetch my Crime Buster Kit, which Lizzie had bought me when I'd first told her I wanted to follow in Dad's footsteps.

Back in the bathroom I laid out all my crime-busting equipment on the floor. As well as my detective-in-training pocket book that gives you lots of hot tips on how to gather evidence, there are several useful pieces of equipment, including a magnifying glass, some sealable plastic 'evidence' bags, a pair of plastic gloves, a fingerprint pad and a stick of chalk for drawing round dead bodies. And I'd recently added a set of tweezers for picking up smaller pieces of evidence, such as broken fingernails or strands of hair, which criminals often leave behind at crime scenes.

I put on the gloves and carefully undid one of the evidence bags. Then I used the tweezers to lift the splinter of wood from the side of the bath and drop it into the bag. Tomorrow I was going to take it into school and see if it matched what was left of the fence. And if it did, I'd have all the proof I needed that my brother was the culprit. *Then* we'd see who was a rubbish detective!

5

But the next morning I totally went off that idea.

For one thing Matthew was clearly terrified about the appointment Dad had made for him with Dr Gregg, and I began to feel sorry for him all over again.

'I was just scared in case you got ill, Matty,' I told him as I watched him standing at the table picking at the breakfast Dad had insisted on making for him. 'Holly said you might get blood poisoning and people can die from that.'

He must have seen how genuinely worried I was because he grunted, 'It's OK, Esmie. Here. Do us a favour and eat some of this will you?' And he shoved his scrambled eggs on toast (which he normally loves) in front of me.

'Hey, it's all going to be over with very quickly, you know,' Dad said, giving him a fatherly pat on the shoulder as he came into the kitchen to make himself a coffee.

'Dad, I don't need to go to the doctor's.'

'I'll take you there on my way to work and I'll drop you off at school afterwards. How's that?'

'Great,' Matthew grunted sarcastically.

'But you might need stitches and then you won't even have to *go* back to school afterwards, will he, Dad?' I said, trying to cheer my brother up.

Matthew and Dad both glared at me then – goodness knows why.

Jake called round as usual to walk Matty to school, and I answered the door because my brother and father were both upstairs. As soon as Jake stepped into our hall it was clear that he had some bad news. He quickly told me that Jennifer had been asked out by another mate of his, called Ian, and that she had agreed to go.

'Oh no! Matty's going to be gutted,' I exclaimed.

Jake didn't have time to tell Matthew about it, because no sooner had my brother come downstairs than there was another ring on our doorbell, and Matthew opened it to find himself face to face with Mr Stevens from across the road.

'I've just come to tell you that your cat has been sitting on my car again,' he told Matthew grumpily. (I should probably mention that Nevada's uncle is just as fussy about his car as he is about his geraniums.)

'Are you sure it wasn't Pixie?' I asked, stepping forward to stand beside Matty.

'No – it was definitely *your* cat because I saw him this morning. I got up early to give my car a wash and the second I'd finished there were muddy paw prints all over it and that Hercules was sitting on the bonnet.' (He pronounced it like the name of the Greek God.)

'His name's *Hercule*,' I corrected him, 'after Hercule Poirot, the famous detective. And he's only a kitten,' I added protectively.

'Yeah, so they can't be very *big* paw prints,' Matthew put in.

Mr Stevens glared at him. 'I suppose you think this is funny.'

'Oh no,' Matthew replied, but he and Jake both sniggered rudely as the two of them brushed past Mr Stevens on their way through the front door.

'Matty, what about the doctor's?' I called after him, but he didn't come back.

Mr Stevens was looking furious. 'I'd like to speak to your father, Esmie – *now*.'

'He's in the bathroom. I'll go and get him.'

When Dad arrived downstairs, Mr Stevens started complaining to *him* about Hercule, who in the meantime had arrived in the hall and was sitting in the middle of the floor, diligently washing his paws.

'I'm sorry, Frank, but I really don't know what I can do about it,' Dad said briskly, looking at his watch. 'You know cats – they have minds of their own. Perhaps you could park your car in the garage in future and then he won't be able to get to it.'

'Ruth's sister's car is in the garage. She's left *that* with us for three months – as well as her daughters!' Clearly Mr Stevens was in a pretty bad mood.

Dad finally managed to get rid of him by advising him to throw water over Hercule if he did it again. (I was horrified, but then Dad can be pretty ruthless sometimes, which I guess comes from dealing with all those murderers at work.)

As he closed the front door he asked me where Matthew was.

'Jake called for him. They've left for school already.'

'He *knew* I was about to drive him to the doctor's.' Dad sighed. 'This is worse than trying to get Hercule in the cat box to take him to the vet.'

'Matty's just nervous cos it's Doctor Gregg,' I told him.

'I know he is, sweetheart, but she's the only one on duty this morning and he needs to get this seen to. Come on. I'll give you a lift to school and we'll try to catch him up.'

In the car I told Dad what Jake had said about Jennifer. 'Matty'll probably be in a really bad mood when you pick him up, Dad.'

Dad sighed. 'Your brother's always in a bad mood these days.'

We had just turned out of our road when I spotted Nevada walking along on her own.

'Dad, there's Nevada,' I told him. 'Can you let me out here please, so I can walk to school with her?'

'I can give you both a lift if you like.'

'No, it's OK. I'd rather walk. Make sure you catch Matty though, won't you?' I climbed out of the car and called out, 'Hi, Nevada!'

She didn't acknowledge me, so I waited for her to catch me up before saying in a rush, 'Listen, I'm really sorry about what happened yesterday. I only told Holly that your mum's a psychic because I think it's really cool. Holly was the one who told everyone else. She's just got a weird sense of humour, that's all.'

'Yeah – and a big mouth,' Nevada snapped.

'Well . . .' I felt torn between agreeing with her and defending Holly – even though she didn't deserve it.

'Still, she's your best mate, right?' Nevada added, almost as if she could read my mind.

I nodded. 'Since we were five.'

'You're lucky. I've always moved around too much to have a best friend.'

'That must be hard,' I said sympathetically. Like I said before, I've lived in the same place all my life, so I don't know what it's like to have to move away from everything and everyone who's familiar to me.

'It's terrible,' she said with feeling.

'But at least you've seen lots of different places,' I pointed out.

'Oh, yeah – I've lived in six different countries so far.' She didn't sound at all enthusiastic about it.

'Holly and I thought you might be American, because of your name,' I told her.

'I was born there.'

'Really? I think America's a really cool place! My grandma lives in Chicago and we've been to visit her twice. Did *you* think it was cool when you lived there?'

'I can't remember – I was only two when we left. Carys was six, so she can remember it, but she always says she can't.' She frowned. 'I sometimes think she just can't be bothered to tell me about it.'

'I know what you mean,' I confided. '*I* can't

remember my mum because she died when I was a baby, whereas Matthew was four, so he can. But whenever I ask him about her, he says he hardly remembers her. I mean, *I* can remember stuff that happened when I was four, so why can't he? I sometimes think he wants to keep her all to himself.'

'It must be awful not having a mum,' Nevada said, sounding sympathetic. 'You know, you should get yourself hypnotized – then you might remember her. My mum says people who get hypnotized can sometimes remember things that happened when they were babies.'

'Yeah . . . well . . .' I didn't feel like pointing out that my mother and I hadn't actually spent any time in the world together at all.

'When I grow up I'd like to *be* a hypnotist,' Nevada continued. 'I think that would be such a cool job.'

'I thought you wanted to be a psychic.'

'Yeah – well that as well.'

We walked along in silence for a bit while I wondered what to say next.

'Does your mum help the police in the way that you said?' I eventually asked. 'You know – sensing where dead bodies are hidden and stuff?' I was thinking how great it would be, if I could tell Holly that Nevada's mum was the sort of psychic who helps find missing people, rather than the kind who tells fortunes at the fair.

Nevada shook her head. 'She's got her own business. People come to her if they've got problems and she tries to help them.'

'What sort of problems?'

'Oh, sometimes they want to know about their love lives, or about relatives who've passed on – stuff like that. She's got contacts in the spirit world and she gets messages from them.'

'Wow!' But before I could question her any further we turned a corner and I spotted Holly in the distance – and so did Nevada, judging by the wary look on her face.

'HOLLY!' I yelled at the top of my voice, thinking that I had to somehow get her and Nevada to spend some time together, so they'd see that there was no reason to dislike each other.

Holly waited for us to catch her up, though she barely even looked at Nevada when we did. 'I just saw Jake,' she informed me. 'He says your dad's taken Matty to see the doctor. I was really worried about him after what you told me last night.'

'Is there something wrong with him then?' Nevada asked.

'It's a secret,' Holly replied quickly. 'Isn't it, Esmie?'

Nevada was scowling, and I thought she might be about to stalk off again, so I said quickly, 'Yes – we'll tell you if you promise not to tell anyone else.'

'Of course I won't,' Nevada said.

So I told her what my brother and Jake had done to the school sign and how Matty had got injured in the process.

'Wow!' Nevada was clearly impressed.

Holly was glaring at me as if I'd just told the whole school instead of only Nevada, so I decided now was a good time to change the subject. 'Jake says that one of his other mates is taking Jennifer out on a date,' I said. 'It's that guy called Ian. You know, Holly, the one who Matty got into a fight with last year when Ian was trying to get Jake and Matty to steal stuff.'

'Who's Jennifer?' Nevada asked.

And before Holly could tell her that *that* was a secret too, I launched into the whole story of my brother's doomed love life and how I'd been trying to think of a way to get him and Jennifer back together because my brother was so miserable without her.

'That's going to be impossible now that Jennifer's found someone else,' Holly declared in an I-told-you-so sort of voice.

'I know,' I agreed gloomily.

'Not necessarily,' Nevada said. 'I mean you could always get Matthew to date someone else too and make sure Jennifer finds out about it.'

'Make her jealous you mean?' Holly sounded scornful. 'It won't work. Jennifer isn't interested in Matthew any more and that's that.'

'Yes, but she might change her mind if she sees him dating a girl who's even more gorgeous than she is,' Nevada pointed out.

'Like who?' I asked. 'Jennifer is pretty attractive, you know.'

'So's my sister.'

'Your *sister*?'

'Sure. Carys was in the driveway the other day when your brother was coming home from school. She said she thought he looked really hot.'

'*Hot*?' I was astounded. Some girls ought to have their eyes tested if you ask me.

Nevada nodded. 'That's what she said.'

'You'd better leave it, Esmie,' Holly warned me. 'Your dad told you he didn't want you interfering in other people's love lives any more, remember?'

'Yeah – but he meant *his* love life, not Matty's,' I replied. 'And if I hadn't interfered in Dad's, then he and Lizzie would never have met, would they?' (Dad and Lizzie met through a Lonely Hearts advert that I placed with the help of the French au pair we had last year – but that's a whole different story.) 'Anyway I know the *real* reason you're telling me to leave it, Holly,' I continued. 'Holly fancies Matthew herself,' I explained to Nevada. 'Goodness knows why!'

Unfortunately Holly reacted like I'd just given away her dearest, for-best-friends'-ears-only personal secret. 'I hate you, Esmie!' she burst out.

And she stomped away in a complete strop, like I had totally betrayed her.

I was horrified, and I was about to rush after her and tell her I was sorry, when Nevada put her hand on my arm. 'Do you want to come round to mine after school and I'll show you some psychic stuff?' she asked.

I immediately stopped thinking about Holly.

'I can read your tea leaves for you if you like,' she added.

I was intrigued. 'Can tea leaves really tell you things about the future?'

'Of course – if you know how to read them properly.'

'And is it *just* tea leaves that you do?'

'How do you mean?'

'Well, you said before that psychics can get

messages from the spirit world, so I was just wondering . . .' I trailed off, feeling self-conscious.

'Were you wondering about contacting your mum?'

'Well . . .' I felt myself flushing. 'It's just that since she's dead, I thought . . .' I broke off nervously. What I was too embarrassed to say was that sometimes when I was younger, I used to think my mother was sending me messages . . . well, not really *messages* . . . more like loving vibes or something . . . from up in heaven. And I used to think I could feel her presence when I looked at her photograph.

'Tell you what.' Nevada was smiling at me encouragingly. 'Why don't I come round to *your* place after school? Then I might get some kind of *sense* of your mum, if you know what I mean. There must still be some stuff in your house that belonged to her, isn't there?'

'Oh yes,' I said. And I immediately remembered the jewellery box.

6

After school Nevada went back to her house to dump her stuff and to tell her aunt she was coming round to mine, and while I was waiting for her I rushed upstairs to fetch my mother's jewellery box. I was excited because I had never met anyone before who believed that dead people could contact you from the spirit world. Dad doesn't believe in spirits or ghosts, or even in heaven, and he thinks it's enough that people who die live on in the memories of others. But then *he* can remember my mother, so it's all right for him.

As I passed my brother's room he opened the door as if he was about to come out, then closed it again abruptly when he saw me. He looked really unhappy and I figured Jake must have told him about Jennifer going out with Ian.

'Did the doctor get that splinter out OK?' I called out to him. 'Did you need any stitches?'

'Go away, Esmie!' he grunted, and I guessed he wouldn't be coming out of his room again until I was gone.

I took the jewellery box downstairs thinking I could show it to Nevada while we were drinking our tea. (I assumed you actually had to *drink* your tea before the tea leaves in the bottom could be read.) I remembered how Holly and I had once tried to read our tea leaves after we'd seen an article about it in one of her mum's magazines. We'd ended up giggling hysterically rather than taking it seriously, and the more I thought about the fun we'd had that time, the worse I felt about falling out with Holly.

Since I still had a few minutes before Nevada arrived, I decided to phone Holly and try and make things up with her, but when I picked up the phone in the living room I found that my brother was already dialling out a number on the upstairs extension.

I guessed he must be phoning Jake, so I got ready to listen in to their conversation. I felt a little bit guilty, but not much. After all, if I was a proper detective I'd be able to get the phone tapped any time I wanted, wouldn't I? (Unless you have to be in MI5 or the FBI or something to do that.)

The phone on the other end of the line

stopped ringing out and a man's voice said, 'Hello?'

'Mr Mitchell, it's Matthew,' my brother said in a nervous voice. 'Can I speak to Jennifer please?'

And that's when I realized he wasn't phoning Jake at all. Since Jennifer hadn't been answering her mobile, he had obviously decided to try her landline instead.

'Jennifer doesn't want to speak to you, Matthew,' her father replied briskly. 'I really don't think there's much point in you phoning her again.'

I waited until Matthew had ended the call, then I went upstairs to meet him as he emerged from Dad's bedroom (which is where the second phone is). A tear was running down his face, which he quickly brushed away when he saw me.

'Oh, Matty, don't cry!' I blurted out.

'I'm *not* crying,' he growled.

I really wanted to comfort him but I couldn't think how, until I suddenly remembered some wise words I'd heard on *EastEnders* recently. They had been uttered by one of the ladies who runs the launderette to one of the other characters after her boyfriend had stolen all her money, poisoned her pet dog and run away to Spain.

'Time is a great healer,' I told Matthew in my wisest voice.

'Oh, shut it, Esmie!' Matty snarled, disappearing into his bedroom and slamming the door.

I sighed, not knowing what else to do.

Just then Hercule came sauntering out of my room, where I guessed he'd been curled up on my bed. I sat down on the floor and stroked him.

'Matty, I'm going to send Hercule in to see you!' I called out to my brother, because whenever *I'm* feeling upset about anything I always find having Hercule around really helps. Since my brother didn't reply, I opened his door and gently pushed Hercule through the gap into his room. Hopefully Hercule would go and curl up against Matthew and purr at him and rub his head against him – which is Hercule's way of telling us that *he* loves us no matter what.

When Nevada arrived, she was holding a small book in her hand called *Tea-Leaf Images and How to Read Them*.

'Great!' I said, as she showed me. But there was something else I wanted to ask her. 'Nevada, you know what you said earlier –

about making Jennifer jealous so she'll want to get back with Matthew . . . ?'

'Yeah?'

'Well I really think we should do it.' I told her about Matty's phone conversation, and how upset he was.

'OK then,' Nevada said. 'You tell Matthew that my big sister really fancies him and wants to go out on a date with him. If he agrees, we'll make sure we get a photo of them together, and then you can show it to Jennifer.'

'What if Matty doesn't want to go out with your sister?' I asked.

'Have you *seen* my sister? She always has loads of boys after her.'

'Then why would she want to go out with my brother?'

'Your brother's pretty nice.'

'No he's not!'

She laughed. 'Trust me, OK? Look, you wait here and I'll go and get a photo of Carys for you to show him. Oh, and make yourself a cup of tea. You should use a cup that's plain white inside.'

As soon as she left I put the kettle on, and I was waiting for it to boil when Jake arrived on his bicycle. 'So how's the broken-hearted one doing, Esmie?' he asked me as I opened the front door to him.

'He's really upset, Jake,' I said.

As we spoke, Nevada's uncle's car was pulling into the driveway across the road and Jake turned to look at it. 'Is that the guy who was complaining about Hercule this morning?'

'Yes. I don't think he likes cats very much.'

Jake went upstairs to my brother's room and I went back into the kitchen to make a cup of tea. We didn't have any loose tea leaves so I had to rip open a tea bag, which I hoped would still have the same effect.

I was just wondering if it was OK to put milk in my tea or not when Nevada arrived back with her sister's photograph. She was right – Carys was stunning. She had a really pretty face and her hair was long and dark like Nevada's, only it looked a lot silkier somehow. She had big dark eyes with long eyelashes and she had a really nice figure too. I couldn't imagine my brother not liking her.

'I've been thinking,' I told Nevada. 'Jennifer does a late shift in Burger King every Saturday. If we can get Matthew to take Carys there, Jennifer will actually *see* them together and we won't have to bother taking a photograph.'

'Great!' Nevada said. 'I know Carys'll be up for that – she loves burgers. Of course we won't tell her his ex-girlfriend works there.'

'I'll show Matthew her photo tonight,' I said. 'Now . . . what about the tea leaves? Oh – and I've got something to show you of my mother's.' I went through to the living room where I had left the jewellery box. 'This belonged to my mother when she was *my* age,' I said, coming back into the kitchen and putting it down on the table in front of Nevada. Do you think you might be able to get what you need from it . . . you know . . . the vibes or whatever . . . ?'

Nevada was staring intently at the box, and for a moment I thought she must be getting psychic vibes off it already. 'I'll need to have it near me for a while and then I'll be able to tell for sure,' she said. She pointed to the cup of tea I had made (in which quite a few tea leaves were visibly floating). 'Start drinking it – but don't rush.'

'Is it all right that I made it with a tea bag?' I asked. 'We don't have any loose tea.'

'Loose tea is better,' Nevada said. 'But don't worry – it will still work.'

I slowly drank my tea, swallowing quite a few tea leaves in the process, as Nevada continued to gaze at the jewellery box as if it was a person whose thoughts she was trying to read.

'Stop when you've got about a teaspoon of liquid left,' she instructed.

'Is this OK?' I asked when I had almost reached the bottom.

'Yes. Now, are you left- or right-handed?'

'Right.'

'OK, so hold the cup in your left hand and move it round in a circle three times. It has to be in an anticlockwise direction. That's it. Now, while you're doing that, concentrate on a question you want the answer to.'

'What sort of question?' I asked.

'Anything. Something you want to know about the future maybe.'

I thought about it for a few moments. Then I closed my eyes and silently I asked, *Am I going to get to speak to my mother?* Of course I knew my mother was dead, but if there was a spirit world like Nevada said . . .

Nevada told me to turn my cup over on to the saucer and let the tea dregs drain away. 'Now you have to leave it like that for a few minutes. In fact I reckon it's best if you spend some time alone with the cup. Why don't you go into another room and shut the door? I'll come and get you when it's time.'

So I took the cup – now upside down on its saucer – out of the kitchen and into the living room.

'Keep thinking about your question,' Nevada called out to me.

So I did, and I was still thinking about it when I heard Matthew and Jake thudding down the stairs. I heard them open the front door and Matthew shouted out – presumably to me – that they'd only be gone for ten minutes. And I sighed with relief because he sounded like he was back to his normal self again.

It felt like ages later when Nevada finally came to get me. She took me back into the kitchen, looking very serious as she instructed me to hold the cup upright again, in my right hand this time.

'Now we can start,' she said, taking hold of my wrist and manoeuvring it so she could look inside the cup herself, peering at it from every angle. Most of the tea leaves had settled into a dense brown sludge on the bottom, but some had also stuck to the side when I had tipped it up. 'See how they thin out towards the rim,' she said. 'I think I'm beginning to see a figure there. Look.'

'I can't see anything,' I said.

'The thinner bit is the face,' she went on. 'That's the eye, that's the nose, that's a moustache and that's the chin. Can you see?'

And the weird thing was that as she pointed

out the individual bits I *did* start to see what she meant. Pretty soon, if I looked at the sludge of wet tea leaves in a certain way, I could see the outline of a face too.

'The thick bit at the bottom, where they're all stuck together, is the body,' she said. 'It's the same size as the head, so you know what that means.'

'What?' I asked, fascinated.

'A short body compared with the head means it's a dwarf.'

'A *dwarf*?' I giggled.

Nevada remained serious. She started to leaf through the book she had brought with her until she got to the 'D' section. '*Dwarf,*' she read out loud. '*A friend in whom you trusted will prove false.*' She looked up at me. 'That's what it means. Look.' She handed the book to me so that I could read it for myself. I had stopped laughing now.

'Who?' I murmured.

Nevada didn't say anything. She was staring again at the jewellery box.

'What is it?' I asked.

'Nothing. I just feel . . . I feel . . .' She slowly put out her hand and cautiously touched the lid as if she was afraid it might give her an electric shock. 'Esmie, I'm getting this really weird feeling.' She turned her head to look me straight in the eyes. 'Was your mother called *Claire*?'

I nodded. 'Yes. How do you know?' I hadn't told her my mother's name and I was almost certain there was nothing visible in our kitchen that could have told her either.

'The name *Claire* just came into my head,' she said solemnly.

And I felt a shiver run down the back of my neck as I looked from her to the box, and back again in disbelief.

7

Jake and Matthew returned just as Nevada was leaving, and they seemed pretty high about something. It was dark and cold outside now and I couldn't think where they'd gone in order to be back in such a short time. I really wanted to tell somebody – even my brother – what had just happened, but Nevada had made me promise not to tell *anyone* or she said she'd have to stop helping me. I still couldn't quite believe that Nevada really *was* psychic, but how else could she have known my mother's name?

As I sat in the kitchen staring at the jewellery box in a kind of daze, my brother and Jake came in to fix themselves some hot drinks. Jake walked across the kitchen to switch on the radio, fiddling with it until he found some music he liked, which he then turned up extra loud.

The plastic clothes-basket was sitting on the

floor by the washing machine and it was full of dry washing waiting to be ironed, some of which was Lizzie's. Jake spotted a pair of pink, lacy knickers and grinned as he held them up to show Matty.

'You'd better put those back,' I said as Jake pulled out a matching camisole top.

'Do you think it suits me?' Jake said, holding Lizzie's camisole against him and wiggling about to the music. He danced over and put the knickers on Matty's head, and my brother left them there, laughing loudly and wolf-whistling at Jake.

'Matty, you'd better stop it,' I warned him. 'Dad's—'

'Dad's gonna kill me, yeah . . . yeah . . . but he's not here, is he?'

'Yeah, Esmie – stop being such a little goody-goody!' Jake teased.

I had been about to tell them that, right at that moment, Dad's car was pulling into our drive (which I knew would be as much of a surprise to Matty as it was to me, since our father hardly ever got home this early). But instead I kept my mouth shut.

As Dad walked in – the sound of his entrance drowned out by the radio – Jake and Matty both had their backs to the door. Jake was still larking about with the camisole and Matty was giggling, the pink knickers still on his head as he bent over and rummaged around in the clothes- basket to see what else was there. Dad stared at them angrily for a few moments, before stepping forward and whacking my brother on the bum (on the *non*-wounded side and not as hard as he might have done, which I guess shows that he's not *that* ruthless).

'Hey!' Matthew protested indignantly, clearly thinking it was me until he turned round and saw Dad glaring at him.

'I told him you'd be mad at him, Dad,' I said brightly, stepping forward to snatch the knickers off my brother's head.

Jake hastily dropped the camisole back in with the other clothes. 'I'm bailing, Matt,' he said quickly. 'See you tomorrow.'

As Jake made a rapid exit, Dad switched off the radio. Then he turned to face my brother, whose hair was standing on end with all the static.

'Dad, we were just mucking around,' Matty blurted. He was blushing bright red now.

'So I see,' Dad snapped. 'And would Jake muck around like that at *his* house, with his *mother's* underwear, do you think?'

Matty opened his mouth but he seemed incapable of further speech.

'He probably would,' I put in helpfully.

'He'd probably muck around like that with his *granny's* underwear. Jake is totally *gross*.'

Dad ignored me and kept his attention fixed on my brother. 'Now you listen to me, Matthew. When Lizzie moves in with us, I expect you to treat her with the same respect you'd treat –' But he broke off then, as if he was suddenly worried that he might have gone too far.

I knew what Dad had been about to say though – and *I* didn't think it was going too far. If you ask me, the trouble with Dad is that he never goes far *enough* where the matter of finding us a new mum is concerned.

'It's a pity Lizzie's *not* really our mother,' I pointed out quickly. 'You know, Dad . . . the way she'd be if you actually got *married* to her . . . Well, she'd be our *step*mother then, not our mother, but that's practically the same thing.' (A couple of weekends ago, Dad had taken Lizzie away for a romantic mini-break and I had got very excited because, according to a survey in one of Holly's mum's magazines, a significantly high proportion of women reported being on a weekend trip away when their partners proposed. But Dad and Lizzie still weren't engaged when they came back, and ever since then I'd been trying to give Dad a bit of a nudge.)

Unfortunately that seemed to make Dad even more irritated. 'Is your homework done, Esmie?' he asked, sounding like he hoped it wasn't so that he could send me off to do it, preferably to the furthest-away room in our house.

'Not exactly, but—'

'Well would you please go and do it *exactly*?' And I ended up getting sent upstairs along with my brother.

I was in the middle of my maths homework when I heard Lizzie arriving, and I was having trouble concentrating because I kept thinking about what had happened earlier with Nevada.

I had brought the jewellery box back up to my bedroom, and the more I thought about it, the harder it was to believe that it could really give out psychic vibes. Of course, it was just possible that Nevada's aunt or uncle had told her my mum's name. They had never known my mum because they had only moved into our street a few years ago, but I supposed that one of our other neighbours could have mentioned her.

As soon as I'd finished the maths problem I was working on, I decided to go and say hello to Lizzie. The living-room door was open and

I could hear Dad and her talking as I descended the stairs.

'So did you get Matthew to the doctor's this morning?' Lizzie was asking.

'Eventually. I guess he's at that really self-conscious sort of age.'

'Unlike Esmie.' Lizzie sounded amused as she added, 'She certainly seems to be enjoying all the drama as usual!'

Dad gave a short laugh. 'I think she's congratulating herself on saving Matty's life!'

'Did Matty say any more about how it happened?'

'No, but I've a feeling it was some prank or other,' Dad replied.

I burst into the room, exclaiming indignantly, 'I am *not* enjoying all the drama!' It was the first time I had ever heard Lizzie say anything about me that was remotely uncomplimentary, and I was a little bit miffed.

'Oh, Esmie, I didn't mean it in a horrible way,' Lizzie said quickly. 'I just meant that you and Holly do always seem to find yourselves at the centre of the action – that's all. Listen, I've got some good news.'

And it turned out that she had just taken a couple to see her flat and they had liked it so much that they'd wanted to rent it as soon as possible. In fact they had even said that they'd prefer to buy it rather than rent it and had offered her a really good price for it.

'That's *brilliant* news!' I exclaimed, beaming at her. Now Lizzie could sell her flat and move in with us and hopefully it wouldn't be long before Dad asked her to marry him.

'Yes, it *is*,' Lizzie said, 'and they totally understood when I told them I'd rather not sell it just yet.'

I felt a tiny pang of worry as I remembered what my brother had said to me the day before. 'Matty says you don't want to sell your flat because you might want to move back into it when you get fed up living with us, but that's not true is it?' I couldn't help blurting out.

Lizzie and Dad both stared at me.

'Matthew said *what*?' Dad said, and I suddenly realized that I might have landed my brother in more trouble.

'John, it's OK,' Lizzie said quickly. 'Matty isn't really himself at the moment.'

Lizzie was a total saint, I thought, though I didn't reckon she'd feel quite so sympathetic towards Matty if she'd seen the way he'd been wearing her knickers on his head earlier on.

'Lizzie's right, Dad,' I said. 'Matty tried to phone Jennifer when we got home from school but she wouldn't speak to him. He was crying afterwards, though he pretended not to be. Holly says boys don't like people to see them cry because they think it's not macho. Do you think that's true, Dad?'

'Well . . .' He looked like he wasn't sure how to respond to that.

'*Holly* reckons boys are really too *afraid* to show their feelings,' I continued, 'whereas girls aren't. She read an article about it in one of her mum's magazines. It was called: *Men versus Women: which is really the weaker sex?*'

Dad rolled his eyes. (He quite often rolls his eyes when I quote things that Holly has said.)

'John, maybe you should go and talk to Matthew now,' Lizzie suggested, sounding worried.

'Sure. I just want to see the news first.'

'It's important that Dad watches the news so that he can keep up to date with all the latest murders,' I told her. 'In fact, I think *I'd* better watch it too.'

Dad sighed impatiently. 'Esmie, have you finished your homework?'

'Not *completely*,' I replied, 'but—'

'Well please go and do it *completely*.'

I sighed too, because Dad can be so predictable sometimes. I left the room like he'd said, but as soon as I reached the stairs I stopped to listen to the rest of their conversation.

'John, he's clearly in a real state over this business with Jennifer.'

'I know he is, but he'll get over it. They've only been dating a few months. I had loads of girlfriends when I was his age.'

'It's not the same. He adored Jennifer. And have you ever thought that he might be more vulnerable than other boys his age when it comes to losing people?'

There was a long pause. 'You mean because he lost Claire?'

'Just go and speak to him, John. Please.'

As I headed for my bedroom I felt puzzled by what Lizzie had said and I wondered if she was right. *Was* Matthew more vulnerable to losing the other people in his life because our mother had died? And if *he* was, did that mean *I* was as well? I remembered that Matthew had been inconsolable for days after our grandmother first moved to Chicago with her new husband. He had been ten at the time, and Dad had had to take time off work to look after him because he'd refused to go to school and refused to stay with our childminder. He had calmed down in the end but he had been very clingy to Dad for a long time afterwards. I had been upset too, of course, but I had got over it much quicker than my brother. And now *I* was the one who was always on the phone to Grandma – not Matthew.

8

The next day was Saturday. Lizzie had gone out, and Dad and I were in the middle of eating breakfast in the kitchen when there was a loud ringing on our doorbell. Dad went to answer it and I followed him.

It was Nevada's uncle, and this time he looked furious.

'If it's about Hercule—' Dad began.

'This morning I found paw prints painted all over the bonnet of my car!'

Dad looked confused. 'When you say *painted*—'

'*Red* paw prints painted all across my bonnet. And I know who's responsible!'

'Look I really don't think Hercule—' Dad began.

'I'm talking about your son! My wife saw him and that friend of his hanging around in the street yesterday evening. That spray-paint doesn't come off, you know. Now my bonnet's ruined and I want to know what you're going to do about it!'

Dad looked astounded. 'Did your wife actually *see* my son spray-painting your car?'

'No, but—'

'Because I find that very hard to believe. He's not a vandal. Look, I'll speak to him and see if he knows anything, but I suggest you make an official complaint down at the police station.'

As Dad closed the front door I looked up the stairs and saw Matthew standing at the top in his pyjama bottoms. He had a surprised sort of expression on his face as if he couldn't believe that Dad had just stood up for him like that.

Dad told him to get dressed and come downstairs. I thought it was a bit strange that Dad wasn't launching into an interrogation straight away, until I realized that he wanted some time to question *me* first.

'Esmie, how long was Jake here yesterday evening?' he asked when we were back in the kitchen with our breakfasts in front of us again.

'Not that long. He just came round to see how Matty was.'

'And did they go outside?'

I nodded. 'But only for a short time.' Not that you needed a long time to spray-paint some paw prints on a car, I thought. I remembered how Matty and Jake had seemed in really high spirits when they'd come back inside again. And there was the even more incriminating fact that they had spray-painted the school sign only a couple of days before, using the same colour paint. But of course, Dad didn't know anything about that.

Matty came downstairs twenty minutes later and stood at the sink munching toast while Dad asked him about Mr Stevens's allegation. He had stopped limping now, but he was still avoiding sitting down whenever possible.

'We did go out the front for a little while last night, but so what?' Matthew said defensively, avoiding meeting Dad's gaze.

'Well, what were you doing out there?' Dad wanted to know.

'Just having a private chat without big-ears listening in,' Matthew answered, looking sideways at me. (And I may as well admit now that that has got to be the most plausible excuse my brother has ever come up with.)

Dad sighed. 'Well, that much I can believe.' He paused. 'So while you were out there, did you see anyone else hanging around?'

'Only Hercule. He had a paintbrush in one paw and a pot of paint hooked over the other. I didn't think anything of it at the time but –' My brother started to giggle.

'Matthew, this isn't funny,' Dad began, although he had the trace of a smile on his face too. 'Look, if you saw anything—'

Just then the doorbell rang again.

Dad sighed. 'If that's Frank I want you to stay out of the way.'

As soon as he left the kitchen, I homed in on my brother. 'It *was* you, wasn't it? It's just like what you did to the school sign!'

Matthew gave an irritating little smirk. 'You can't prove anything, Esmie – and neither can Dad.'

'It's for you, Esmie!' Dad shouted from the hall.

I immediately thought it must be Holly coming to make up with me, and I hurried to the front door.

It was Nevada. 'Esmie, I need to speak to you in private.'

I led her up to my room, where I quickly straightened my duvet and pulled back the curtains. 'Your uncle just came over here about his car,' I said.

Nevada nodded. 'He's really furious about it. He's phoned the garage and he has to report it to the police or he won't be able to claim on his insurance. He wanted to give them Matthew's name, but Aunt Ruth's made him promise not to. She didn't actually *see*

Matthew do it, and she doesn't want to fall out with your dad as well as with Mrs Lewis.' She paused. 'The thing is, even if your brother *did* do it, Carys isn't going to hold it against him. She really wants to go out with him on a date. That's what I came to tell you.'

'I haven't even shown Matthew her photo yet,' I said.

'Well, you'd better hurry up. I'll give you her mobile number, and if he wants to meet her, tell him to text her. He can't call at the house or Uncle Frank will have a fit.'

'I'll tell him,' I said.

As Nevada was leaving my room she noticed the photograph that always stands on my dressing table.

'Is that your mum?' she asked.

'Yes.'

'Can I touch it?'

I nodded, starting to feel the back of my neck go tingly as she picked up the photograph and ran her finger gently across the glass covering my mother's face.

'Can I have another look at jewellery box?'

I nodded again and watched her carefully pick that up too, lifting the lid to reveal the inside, which was still totally empty. Somehow I hadn't been able to bring myself to fill it with my own jewellery yet.

'It's just that I've been getting some other names in my head,' she said softly. 'I'm not sure if they were friends of your mum or something. The names are Rusty . . . Kirsten . . . and Amanda . . .'

I frowned. We were still in touch with quite a few of my mother's friends and none of them were called that. 'I don't think so,' I said.

'Well, those are the names I'm getting. They must have been her friends when she was younger or something. You said this was her jewellery box when she was your age, didn't you?'

'Yes, but . . .' I trailed off. To be honest I was starting to feel a bit sceptical about Nevada's psychic skills. After all, it was easy enough to pluck three names out of the air and tell me they must have been my mother's friends when she was a girl. I mean, how could I ever prove or disprove that?

Nevada seemed to sense how I was feeling. 'If you don't believe me, you should ask someone who knew your mum as a child,' she said. 'Has she got any brothers or sisters?'

'My grandma in America would be the best person,' I said. 'She'd know the names of the friends my mum had when she was my age.'

'Ask her then.'

'I will.'

'And don't forget to ask Matthew about Carys. She's not doing anything tonight if he wants to take her out.'

'Tonight?'

'It's Saturday. Isn't that when you said Jennifer works at Burger King?'

I nodded. Nevada had a point. 'I'll ask him today,' I said.

'Hey, do you want to come and have a look at my uncle's car?' she added as an after-thought.

So I went outside with her and had a look. On the car's shiny white bonnet, two sets of paw prints had been sprayed, not very neatly, in bright red paint.

'It isn't that funny, is it?' she said. 'Especially since it won't wash off.'

'It's not funny at all,' I agreed. And suddenly I felt really ashamed of my brother.

When I got back to our house I went straight up to Matty's room. 'You've made a real mess of Mr Stevens's car, Matthew,' I told him. 'Now he's got to take it to the garage and get the bonnet totally resprayed, and it's going to cost loads of money.'

'Look, Esmie, it's got nothing to do with you,' he grunted.

'Yes it has,' I replied. 'I don't want to watch

you turn into a criminal and get sent to prison, OK?'

'Esmie, don't be daft!'

'You just broke the law, Matthew!' I snapped. 'And if you don't promise not to do anything like this again, then I'm going to tell Dad. I reckon *he'll* know how to make you stop.'

'Hey, come off it, Ez!'

'Well, promise me then.'

'OK, OK, I promise. Look, Jake and I got a bit carried away last night, that's all.'

'Lizzie's right,' I said crossly. 'You're *not* yourself and it's all because of Jennifer. But that's no excuse! You've got to either get her back or get over her! Here!' And I thrust the photo of Carys into his hand, telling him that she had already spotted him from across the road, and that she fancied him and wanted to go out on a date with him.

When he had finished gaping at me, he looked at the photo and I could tell he was impressed with Carys's looks. 'The thing is, Esmie,' he said, handing it back to me, 'I don't think I *can* go out with anyone else at the moment.'

'Listen, Matthew, if you take Carys to Burger King tonight it might make Jennifer jealous enough to want you back.'

He frowned. 'I couldn't do that.'

'Why not? If you want her back, isn't it worth trying anything?'

'I don't know, Esmie.' He sniffed. 'Look, when she broke up with me she said I wasn't mature enough – that she wanted to go out with somebody older. So that's Ian – not me.'

'Ian's only a couple of years older than you,' I said. 'And anyway, he's totally gross.'

'Jennifer doesn't seem to think that.'

'Well, she might after she's actually gone out with him on a date,' I said. 'Look, Matthew it's up to you . . . but Carys says to text her if you want to take her out tonight. Her number's on the back of the photo. Oh – and apparently she *loves* burgers.'

While Dad and I were washing up the breakfast things, I asked him if it was OK for me to phone my grandma in Chicago that afternoon.

He nodded. 'But for goodness sake don't wake her up at five in the morning like you did the last time.' (The UK is six hours ahead of Chicago and I have a bad habit of forgetting that.) 'I'm going to meet Lizzie in town later,' he continued. 'Your brother can stay here with you until I get back.'

'Aren't I allowed to come too?'

'Not this time. I'm taking Lizzie out to lunch.'

'Is it a romantic lunch?' I asked hopefully.

He sighed. 'Sometimes Lizzie and I like to have some time to ourselves, Esmie, that's all.'

But I was thinking about that article in Holly's mum's magazine that had surveyed all the places where different readers' marriage proposals had occurred. Near the top of the list, just behind romantic weekends away, had been romantic meals in restaurants – especially if the restaurant held some kind of special significance for the couple concerned.

'*I* know!' I told him excitedly. 'Why don't you take her to that nice French restaurant – the one where you and Lizzie first met?'

'That *was* a nice restaurant,' he agreed.

'You should book a table,' I told him. And I rushed off to look up the number in the telephone directory before he could change his mind.

I was so desperate to phone my grandmother that when two o'clock came (which meant it would be eight in the morning in Chicago) I couldn't hold off any longer.

The phone rang out a few times before Grandma answered. She didn't sound too sleepy so I guessed I probably hadn't woken her up.

'Hi, Grandma, it's me – Esmie!'

'Esmie! Ah!' She sounded pleased, and we chatted for a while about all the usual things, including the fact that she and my step-grandad were coming to stay with us for Christmas. Then I told her I had something to ask her about my mother. 'Grandma, I was wondering if you could remember the names of any of the friends she had when she was my age.'

'What a funny question, Esmie. Now let me think . . . Her best friend in primary school was called Heather. Then there was Theresa who lived round the corner from us. There were several others, but—'

'What about Rusty or Kirsten or Amanda?' I interrupted her.

'Oh, well . . . yes . . . Kirsten and Amanda were the girls we knew in Brighton.'

I was so surprised I couldn't speak. So Nevada hadn't been making it up.

'How on earth did you find out about them?' Grandma asked, sounding curious.

'Oh, it's just something someone . . . um . . . told me . . .' I mumbled.

'Something *who* told you?'

I knew I couldn't tell her the truth, and I

also knew I had to come up with some sort of explanation fast. 'Dad's been clearing some stuff out of the loft and there were things up there that belonged to my mum, so . . . so we've been talking about her. He gave me a jewellery box that belonged to her too.'

'That big wooden box, you mean?'

'Yes.'

'Oh, she loved that. It was the girls in Brighton who gave it to her!'

'Really?' I exclaimed. 'That's . . . that's . . .' I was speechless because it was all making perfect sense now – well, perfect *psychic* sense at least. I started to feel a bit trembly, as if I needed to lie down.

'It's all a very long time ago, that's what it is,' Grandma said, sighing. 'Still, it's important to remember the past.' And without me even asking, she began to tell me about the many summers she and my mother had spent in Brighton. 'You see, one of my sisters – Esmerelda, who *you* were named after of course – had a holiday flat there. She used to let us use it whenever we wanted, so I often took your mother there for the whole of the summer holidays. Kirsten and Amanda were a similar age to your mother and they lived in the flat next door – a very nice family. They had a dog too – oh, I believe the dog was called

Rusty! Anyway, the girls got along famously. They even invented their own club.'

'What sort of club?'

'Oh, they called themselves the Adventurous Four or the Famous Four – something like that. It was all very hush-hush. Your mother was very like you in a lot of ways, Esmie. She liked her secrets!'

'Was she a bit of a drama queen as well?' I asked.

Grandma laughed. 'She certainly could be at times!'

When I came off the phone, I went and lay down on my bed, thinking about what my grandmother had told me and how, when Holly and I were younger, we had invented our own secret club too. We had turned the empty shed at the bottom of Holly's garden into our headquarters, and Holly's mum had made us a yellow curtain to pull across the window whenever we were having one of our secret meetings. We'd even made up our own club song, which we'd sing at the start of every meeting:

We have a club, a very cool club,
And we are the members o-of it,
We're loyal and true and wise and good,
Just like the members of a club should.

(OK, so it went a bit weird at the end, but we were only eight at the time and we thought the main thing was to make it rhyme.)

I found myself wondering if my mum and her friends had had a club song and, if so, whether it had been nearly as daft as ours. And I smiled, because even though my mother wasn't around to tell me all the things she'd done as a child, it seemed like I was still managing to follow in her footsteps a little bit.

9

I knew I had to tell Nevada that she'd been right about those names, and I reckoned I ought to tell her sooner rather than later. After all, I'd been pretty disbelieving when she'd come round earlier.

I hurried across the road to the Stevens's place and rang the bell, hoping that Nevada's uncle wasn't going to be the one who answered the door. His car was gone from the driveway, so hopefully that meant he was out.

The door was answered by Nevada's sister, Carys, who I recognized straight away from her photo, though she looked smaller and younger in real life. Her hair was gorgeous – long, black and straight – but she was wearing jeans and a baggy jumper rather than a figure-hugging dress, and she didn't have any make-up on.

'Hi,' I said. 'I'm Esmie from across the road.'

I thought of adding, 'Matthew's sister,' but decided against it. 'Is Nevada in?' I asked.

She nodded. 'I'll get her.' She yelled up the stairs, 'NEVADA!'

Nevada appeared at the top of the stairs and motioned for me to come up.

'Where are your aunt and uncle?' I asked, because there didn't seem to be any sign of them.

'Aunt Ruth's gone to the shops and Uncle Frank's at the garage with his car. They won't be back for a bit.'

She led me into her bedroom, which had flowery paper on the walls, an old-fashioned wardrobe and dressing table, and a double bed with a frilly bedspread. The dressing table was cluttered with Nevada's things, and there were a couple of cuddly toys lying on a chair. But otherwise, apart from a pile of CDs stacked up next to a pretty funky-looking portable CD player, the room didn't really look like it belonged to a girl my age.

'A lot of my stuff's gone into storage,' she said, seeing me looking round. 'Mum didn't want us to clutter up Aunt Ruth's house too much, since we aren't going to be here for that long. So . . . ?' She paused expectantly.

'Has Carys said any more to you about Matthew?' I asked, quickly.

She nodded. 'He sent her a text and she texted him back. They're going to Burger King at six o'clock tonight.'

'He actually asked her out?'

'Well, I think *she* asked *him* in the end, but he suggested Burger King and she agreed. I guess Jennifer will be there, won't she?'

'Yes!' I took a deep breath, suddenly feeling nervous about telling her the main reason for my visit. 'Nevada . . .' I began. 'You know those names you gave me . . . the ones you said were my mum's friends when she was my age . . . well, I phoned my grandma and she said they were the same friends who gave my mother that jewellery box. They were called Amanda and Kirsten, and their dog was called Rusty.'

'Told you so!' Nevada started to smile.

'I know,' I said. 'It's spooky isn't it?'

'Not really. I told you I was psychic, didn't I?'

'Yes, but . . .' I trailed off.

'But you didn't believe me?'

'Sorry,' I murmured. I paused. 'Nevada . . . does this mean . . . does this mean you can put me in touch with my mother?'

She looked at me very seriously. 'I'm not sure . . . but if you wait a minute, there's something I can try right now.' She went over to the wardrobe and opened it. 'My mum doesn't know I've got this,' she said, crouching down to lift something out of the bottom, which she had hidden behind her shoes. When she turned round again I saw that she was holding a crystal ball.

'Wow!' I gasped. 'Is it real?'

'Of course! It's my mum's spare one.'

I stared at the glass ball in awe. 'Can I touch it?'

'Sure. You can hold it if you like. It won't respond to you though.'

She handed the ball to me and I was surprised by how heavy it was. The glass inside was flecked with different colours, and looking into it was like peering inside a miniature glass universe.

'OK, put it down on the floor,' she told me, and as I carefully placed it on the carpet, she sat down cross-legged in front of it. 'Sit opposite me,' she instructed.

I watched her stretch out both hands, palms downwards, so they were almost touching the crystal ball. She was frowning and peering into it as if she was searching for something, then she lowered her hands and touched the surface of the glass very lightly with her fingers.

She sat there for ages not saying anything while I stared at her in awe.

'I see a wedding,' she finally said.

I gasped. 'Really? Is it Dad and Lizzie's?'

'I see a white dress, confetti, a church . . .'

I frowned. 'Dad said once that if he and Lizzie ever *do* get married it will probably be in a registry office.'

'It might not be a church – it could be another sort of building. There's a ring – a gold ring. Everyone's happy . . .'

'*When* is it?' I asked.

'It's in your future. It could be in your near future or in your distant future – but there's a wedding there definitely.' She had taken her hands away from the crystal ball now. 'That's all it's telling me.'

'But that's brilliant!' I exclaimed. 'I really want Dad and Lizzie to get married. It must be *their* wedding!'

Nevada nodded. 'It could be.'

Suddenly we heard the front door closing and Nevada's aunt calling out, 'I'm home, girls!'

'Quick,' Nevada said, jumping up. 'She'll go mad if she finds me showing you this. *She* thinks it's a load of rubbish.'

By the time Mrs Stevens had come up the stairs, the crystal ball was safely back in the wardrobe, and Nevada and I were sitting on the bed flicking through a magazine – which just happened to contain several photos of a celebrity's wedding. There was one picture that I especially liked, so Nevada tore it out for me.

'I'd better go,' I said, looking at my watch. 'Dad and Lizzie will be back soon.'

'Let's keep our fingers crossed about tonight,' Nevada said.

'What's happening tonight?' Mrs Stevens asked as she put her head round the door to see what we were doing.

'Oh, Carys is going out on a date, that's all,' Nevada said quickly.

'Really? With who?'

'It's just some boy she's met since we moved here.'

'How can she have met any boys here? She scarcely leaves the house.'

'She was going to tell you about it, Aunt Ruth,' Nevada replied. 'It's just that you've been a bit tied up this morning, what with Uncle Frank's car.'

'I'd really better go,' I said quickly. 'See you later.' And I made a hasty exit before the conversation about Nevada's uncle's car and Carys's date could progress any further.

As I crossed the street back to my own house, I wondered if Matthew had told Dad about his date tonight yet. It wasn't as if Dad was likely to object – now that Matty's sixteen, Dad gives him a lot more freedom, especially at the weekends – but he does always insist that Matthew tells him exactly where he's going. And if Matty mentioned Burger King, Dad might get suspicious, because he knows Jennifer works there on Saturdays.

Just as I was thinking I'd better warn Matty about that, Dad's car turned into our street and I was instantly distracted by my eagerness to know the outcome of Dad and Lizzie's lunch.

I was waiting in the hall when they stepped in through the front door, and the first thing I did was look at the third finger of Lizzie's left hand – the finger where an engagement ring would be if Dad had just given her one. After all, Nevada's crystal ball had seemed pretty positive on the subject of weddings.

There was no ring – and Dad and Lizzie didn't even ask why I was staring so pointedly at Lizzie's hand – but I didn't let that put me off. 'Well?' I asked as they took off their coats. 'Did you have a nice time? Did anything *exciting* happen while you were there?'

'Lizzie found a hair in her French omelette,' Dad said. 'That was quite exciting. I'm not sure we'll be eating there again though.'

'We had a lovely time, thank you, Esmie,'

Lizzie said, frowning at Dad as if she thought he might have offended me, since the choice of restaurant had been my idea. (Lizzie is quite sensitive that way – unlike Dad.)

'I was reading a magazine while you were out and there's something in it I want to show you,' I told them, taking the page Nevada had given me out of my pocket and unfolding it. I had been hoping I wouldn't need to use the picture, but it was becoming increasingly clear to me that dropping hints with my usual subtlety just wasn't going to do the trick.

'Look, Dad – I've seen this really lovely dress!' I said, handing it to him. 'I think this colour would really suit me, don't you?'

I watched Dad's face very closely to see how he would react, but he just stared at it dumbly as Lizzie moved across to look at the picture too.

'See you later!' I sang out, racing upstairs.

Like I said before, my subtler hints just didn't seem to be working – which was why I had shown them a photograph of a really gorgeous bridesmaid's dress.

I went straight to my brother's room and knocked loudly. When he didn't answer, I tried to go in, but found that I couldn't, and since none of our bedrooms has a lock I guessed he must have pushed something against the inside of the door.

'Matty, let me in! I want to talk to you!' I called out.

There was no reply, though I could hear him moving about inside.

'Dad says we're not allowed to block the doors to our rooms,' I reminded him. 'He says it's a potential fire risk.'

'Yeah, well, Dad thinks everything is a risk,' Matty grunted, sounding miserable.

'Matty, what's wrong?' I asked, genuinely concerned now.

I heard him moving something away from the door, and when he opened it his eyes were red and puffy as if he had been crying again.

'Oh, Matty, it's going to be OK,' I said, darting forward to give him a hug.

'But I've arranged this date with Carys, and now I just feel even worse,' Matthew said, actually letting me embrace him for a few seconds before shaking me off. 'I don't think I can go through with it, Esmie.'

'Of course you can go through with it,' I said firmly. 'You're going to make Jennifer really jealous tonight – you'll see! Anyway, the date with Carys is all set up now, isn't it?'

'Yeah,' he admitted.

I lowered my voice. 'But you'd better not tell

Dad you're going to Burger King. He knows Jennifer works there and he might think you're just taking Carys there to cause trouble.' I was about to add that maybe it wasn't a great idea to mention that his date *was* with Carys.

Matthew sighed. 'Look – maybe I shouldn't go there at all. If Jennifer fancies Ian, then maybe I just have to accept that.'

'She can't fancy him *that* much. He's got red hair, and Holly says that girls hardly ever fancy boys with red hair.'

To my surprise he actually laughed. 'Yeah, well, we all know Holly talks a load of rubbish!' But her rubbish seemed to have cheered him up, because he added, 'I guess I shouldn't give up without a fight, huh? I'd better go and tell Dad before he books me in for babysitting duties tonight.'

I followed him downstairs and listened as he told our father about his date. 'We'll probably go and get something to eat in the High Street, OK?'

'Fine.' Dad was clearly delighted that Matthew had finally stopped moping over Jennifer. 'Who's the lucky girl then?'

'Carys, from across the road,' Matthew replied before I could stop him.

Dad looked puzzled. 'Ruth and Frank's niece, you mean?'

'Yeah.'

'I'm surprised they're letting you take her out. Frank seemed pretty convinced that you were the one who vandalized his car.'

Matthew shrugged. 'Yeah, well, I guess he must have come to his senses.'

'Well, I hope so, because I'd hate this to be a repeat of when you first started going out with Jennifer.' (When my brother and Jennifer had first started dating, Jennifer's dad had done everything he could to stop them – but that's a story for another time.)

'Look, Dad, I'm not *going out* with Carys, OK?' Matty said. 'I'm just taking her for a burger. Or pizza,' he added swiftly.

'Well, I think that's a very sensible attitude. And I think it's great that you're getting yourself back out there.' Dad patted him on the back approvingly.

'Get off, Dad,' Matty said, squirming away. 'God, you're so embarrassing sometimes.'

And he headed back upstairs and shut himself in his room again.

10

I was still up when my brother came home that evening, so I followed him into his room and demanded to know all about his date.

'Was Jennifer there? Did you speak to her?' I blurted excitedly, hurling myself on to his bed and getting ready to grab hold of the headboard if he tried to eject me.

Matty was looking tired and I guessed he didn't have the energy to argue. 'Yes, she was there. But so was Ian. He kept going over and talking to her when she wasn't serving anyone. And when she gave him his burger he gave her a kiss.'

'Oh dear,' I said.

'Yeah – and Carys wants to go out to the cinema with me next week, so now I've got to deal with that as well.'

'Did Carys see Jennifer?' I asked.

'Yeah – but she didn't know who she was. Look, Esmie, I want to go to bed now, OK?'

I looked at my watch. Matty had come home well before his curfew and it still wasn't all that late. 'You don't have to pretend you're going to bed, just to get me to leave your room, you know.'

'I'm not pretending,' Matthew said. 'Just get out, will you?'

Suddenly I noticed something. 'Where's your photo?' I asked him.

Matty has a photo of our mother in his bedroom, just like I do, and usually he keeps it on top of his desk.

'I put it away.'

'Why?'

'I just did. Now get out Esmie or I'm fetching Dad.'

I figured my brother must be seriously exhausted if he needed Dad's help to get me out of his room, so I decided to leave him to it.

The next morning I went downstairs to find Matty and Lizzie arguing in the kitchen. Lizzie was telling Matty not to drink straight out of the orange-juice carton.

'You're not my mother,' Matty said between glugs. 'You can't tell me what to do.'

Lizzie sounded impatient. 'I know I'm not your mother, but that doesn't mean I want your saliva in my orange juice.'

I walked into the kitchen and asked, 'Where's Dad?'

'In the shower,' Lizzie answered without moving her gaze from my brother, who was still taking defiant swigs just to annoy her. And suddenly I couldn't help thinking about our real mother, and wondering what *she* would have done in this situation. (Juliette, our au pair, once told me that dead mothers always deal with everything perfectly because they only have to do it in your imagination – and that it's much harder to be a live one. And as I watched Lizzie glaring at my brother, I reckoned it must be especially hard to be a live one that's taking the place of a dead one.)

Lizzie got up abruptly and said she was going to eat her breakfast somewhere else if Matthew was going to be so revolting, and after she'd gone I hissed, 'Matty – if you still want Lizzie to be our new mum, then you'd better stop being so horrible to her.'

'*Step*mum,' he corrected me, putting the juice back in the fridge. 'We've already got a mum. She just happens to be pretty useless, since she's dead.'

I gasped. 'That's a horrible thing to say!'

I made myself some toast and made a point of taking it into the living room to eat with

102

Lizzie. 'Sorry about Matty,' I told her. 'He can be a real pig sometimes.'

She gave me a weak smile. 'Well, there's a lot going on for him right now, Esmie, what with me moving in and Jennifer breaking up with him.'

'It's not just you he's angry with,' I told her. 'He's put our mother's photograph away as well, and he says she's useless because she's dead.' (Somehow I really wanted to get that off my chest – plus I thought it would be good for Lizzie to know that she wasn't the only target for my brother's stroppiness.)

'Really?' Lizzie sounded even more concerned.

She must have been worried enough to tell Dad everything, because later he went upstairs to speak to my brother, and since I was upstairs too, I decided to listen in.

'Matthew, you're going to wear yourself out – and the rest of us – if you carry on like this,' I heard Dad say as I crouched down outside the door.

'Carry on like *what*?' my brother grunted.

'You know what.'

Matty didn't answer, so Dad continued, 'Look, I know it feels like the end of the world right now, but Jennifer was your first girlfriend and you're only sixteen. I reckon you'll go out with a lot more girls before you find the right one.'

'I don't want to go out with any other girls,' Matty said.

'Just give yourself some time. Time *does* heal, you know. It's the biggest cliché in the book, but it's true.'

There was an awkward-sounding pause, as if Matty wasn't buying that any more than when *I'd* said it to him.

After a bit, Dad asked, 'What have you done with your mother's photograph?'

'It's in the drawer,' Matthew said. He sounded angry as he added, 'It's not as if a picture makes a difference.'

Dad sighed. 'Matty, your mother would have given anything not to have had to leave you. She loved you very much.'

'So?'

'What do you mean, *so?*' Dad sounded like he was the one who was getting cross now. 'Matthew, your mother was thirty-one years old when she died. She had everything to live for. She never even got to *see* Esmie. There's no "*so?*" about it!'

Matty murmured something that I couldn't hear and it was at that moment that the doorbell rang and I was forced to abandon my position.

I quickly went downstairs to see who it was and, as Lizzie opened the door and invited our visitor inside, I saw to my amazement that it was Jennifer.

'Hi, Jen,' Matty mumbled. He had come downstairs to greet her in the hall and I could tell he was really nervous.

Jennifer looked nervous too. 'Hi, Matthew. Listen, I'm sorry I couldn't speak to you properly last night.' She glanced over to where I had sat myself down on the bottom stair to listen (whereas Dad and Lizzie had tactfully removed themselves to the kitchen). 'Matty, I really need to speak to you in private. Can we go outside?'

'Sure.'

Dad must have been listening too, because as soon as they'd shut the front door behind them, he came out into the hall and said, 'I thought he went out with Carys last night.'

'He did.'

'So what did Jennifer mean about not getting the chance to speak to him?'

I decided the best thing to do was plead ignorance, so I just shrugged and said I was going up to my room.

Ten minutes later I heard Matty come bursting in through the front door, and he was whooping with delight as he charged up the stairs.

'Well?' I demanded, going to meet him on the landing. 'Does she want you back?'

'Yeah! She says that seeing me with Carys last night made her realize how stupid she'd been!'

'Matty, that's brilliant!' I felt like dancing with excitement. 'Can I go across the road and tell Nevada?'

He nodded. 'There's just one problem though.'

'Is it Carys?' I asked.

'No – it's Ian. Apparently he got really mad when Jennifer phoned him this morning to let him know she wanted to get back with me. He told her he was going to come round here and sort me out.'

I instantly stopped feeling so good. 'We'd better tell Dad.'

'No way are we telling Dad! Look, Ian's probably all mouth – but if he shows up, I'll deal with him, OK?'

'But, Matthew—'

'It'll be all right, Ez, I promise. Just *please* don't mention this to Dad.'

So I promised I wouldn't, although I was still pretty worried.

I went over to Nevada's house to tell her the

news, and this time her aunt answered the door to me. 'Hello, Esmie. Nevada's upstairs. Go up if you want.'

So I went up and found Nevada sitting cross-legged on her bed, looking through a photograph album. She was looking sad so I guessed she might be looking at photos of her mum and dad, but she cheered up when she saw me and closed the album with a bang. 'So?' she asked. 'Did it work?'

'Yes,' I answered triumphantly. 'Jennifer just came round and she wants to get back with Matty. He's really happy.'

She smiled. 'That's great. It's a shame Carys likes him so much, but I can just tell her he got back with his old girlfriend. She'll get over it.'

I nodded, feeling a momentary pang of remorse for involving Carys in our scheme – but then Carys was so beautiful that she could easily do a lot better than my brother (who really does have an incredibly spotty back).

'Esmie, I had a dream about your mother's jewellery box last night,' Nevada said. 'It was as if your mother was trying to tell me something.'

'What?' I asked.

'I'm not sure exactly, but in the dream the box had something hidden inside it.'

'Like a piece of jewellery, you mean?'

'No, it looked like a piece of paper . . . maybe a message.'

'A message?' I could feel the hairs on the back of my neck prickling.

'I think so. Maybe you'd better have another look in that box.'

'But people can dream anything,' I pointed out. 'I mean, *I* dream weird stuff all the time and it doesn't mean it's true.'

'Psychic people are different,' Nevada said firmly, and she fixed me with her most piercingly intense gaze, as if she could read not only *my* mind but the minds of all my dead ancestors as well.

As I left Nevada's house I started to feel excited about what she'd told me. Was it possible that the jewellery box really *did* contain some sort of message from my mother?

I remembered how, when I was much younger, I used to imagine that the picture frame that holds my mother's photograph – the one that's been in my bedroom for as long as I can remember – might have some sort of message inside. I had even opened it up once to look behind the photo, but of course there hadn't been anything there.

'Hey, you!' someone shouted as I crossed the road.

I looked up to see Ian perched on his bicycle in front of our house. I hadn't seen him in a while, but I recognized him easily because of his hair.

He must have noticed that I looked alarmed, because he grinned and said, 'Don't worry. I don't hurt little girls. Just give your brother a message from me. Tell him to expect trouble. OK?'

'My dad's a policeman and if you hurt Matthew he'll have you arrested,' I told him defiantly.

Ian just laughed. 'I don't think so, sweetheart.' And he turned his bike round and left.

I watched to make sure he cycled right out of our road, then I ran up the drive to our front door.

But as soon as I stepped inside the house I knew something was wrong. I could hear Dad shouting at my brother in the living room, and as I shut the front door behind me, Lizzie came out from the kitchen.

'What's happened?' I asked her.

'Your dad just found a can of spray-paint in the outside bin,' she told me, sounding very worried. 'And it's the same colour that was used on Mr Stevens's car.'

11

Matty was denying everything, which probably meant that Dad's interrogation was still in its early stages. (I've never known our father not to succeed in getting to the truth eventually whenever Matty's done something wrong.)

'Esmie, do you know anything about this?' Dad pointed to the aerosol can of red spray-paint that was sitting on the coffee table.

I shook my head.

'Strangely enough, neither does your brother.' Dad turned back to Matthew, fixing him with an icy look.

'I don't see why you have to assume it's mine,' Matty grunted.

'Well, if it doesn't belong to me or Lizzie, and Esmie doesn't know anything about it, then that only leaves you, doesn't it?'

'So how come just cos Esmie says it's not hers, you believe *her* straight away?' Matthew demanded.

'Call it my policeman's intuition,' Dad said. 'And the fact that you've never been any good at lying ever since you were a little boy.'

Matty flushed and looked like he was about to cave in, even though *I* knew Dad was bluffing. (Detectives do that a lot to try and get their suspects to confess and I could tell Matty was about to fall straight for it.)

That's when I had my brainwave. (Like I said before, I have a real weakness for wanting to help Matty when he's in major trouble with Dad.)

'I bet *I* know who put it there!' I announced.

Dad and Matthew both stared at me.

'I just met Ian outside! You know, Dad – the ginger-haired guy who Matty got into that fight with last year. Anyway, Jennifer's just dumped *him* to get back with Matty. He told me to warn Matty to expect trouble. Well, this must be it! What if *he* planted that can in our bin? I mean he had motive *and* opportunity, didn't he?' (Our wheelie bin stands at the side of our house and it's easy enough for anyone to walk up our drive to it.)

Dad looked sceptical. 'Why would Ian want to spray-paint Frank's car? He doesn't even know him.'

'But he knows *Matty* knows him,' I pointed

out. 'And he knows Matty would get the blame.'

Dad was frowning. 'There *was* a boy with red hair hanging about in the street when I went out to the bin just now.' He turned to look at my brother. 'Do you think this could be true – that Ian painted Frank's car?'

Matty looked bewildered. 'I don't know.'

'When did Jennifer tell Ian she was ditching him and getting back with you?'

'Last night,' Matty said.

'You mean *Friday* night, Matty,' I corrected him swiftly, seeing where this was leading, 'which is why, on *Friday* night Ian must have painted Mr Stevens's car, knowing you would get the blame. And *this* morning Ian must have planted that paint can in our bin, to make sure you did.'

'Oh, yeah,' my brother agreed, though he still looked like he hadn't totally caught up with me.

Dad's face was unreadable as he asked, 'Does either of you know this Ian's address?'

Matty looked alarmed. 'Why do you want to know his address?'

'Because I want to speak to him.'

'Dad, this isn't some police case you have to investigate,' Matty protested.

'No, but I want the person who spray-painted Mr Stevens's car to face the consequences,' Dad replied crisply. 'And from where I'm standing, if it wasn't Ian, it was you. So is there anything else you want to tell me?'

Matty shook his head, looking very pale all of a sudden. 'Jake'll know his address,' he said in a small voice.

'Good. Well, call him now, please.'

Luckily for my brother, Jake's phone was engaged, so Matthew had to leave a message on the voicemail asking him to phone back. In the meantime, I went up to my bedroom and closed the door. What with all this fuss about the paint can, I hadn't had the chance yet to find out if what Nevada had said about my mother's jewellery box was true. It seemed so unlikely that I didn't want to get my hopes up, but still . . .

Taking a deep breath, I picked up the jewellery box, sat down on my bed with it and opened it up. First I lifted out the upper tray and checked underneath that, just in case there was a piece of paper or something stuck to the bottom that I hadn't noticed before. There wasn't, so I carefully inspected the lower section of the box. There didn't seem to be anything hidden under the material that lined the floor, and nothing rattled when I turned the whole box upside down and shook it.

I sat for a few minutes, trying to think what to do next. Whenever detectives on television are searching for a secret compartment (if there's a dead body hidden behind a wall for instance) they always tap on the wall to see if it's hollow anywhere. I turned the box over again and rapped on the base of it with my knuckle. It did sound hollow, but then boxes *are* hollow, so that didn't help much either.

I spent a bit more time shaking the box from every angle, tapping the wood repeatedly and trying in vain to find any holes in the lining. But in the end I found nothing, and I could only conclude that, this time, Nevada had been mistaken. There was no secret message from my mother. And to my surprise I suddenly felt quite angry with Nevada for leading me to believe that there might be.

There was no time to feel too upset however, because a few minutes later Dad shouted up the stairs, 'Matthew! Esmie! Come down here!'

I met my brother on the landing.

'Why did you dump that paint can in *our* bin?' I hissed at him. 'Honestly, Matty – you'd make a rubbish criminal!' (I reckon if my brother murdered someone he'd leave the murder weapon covered in blood on his own front doorstep.)

'Yeah, well I didn't think Dad would go nosing around in there, did I?' he hissed back.

We stared at each other then, both thinking the same thing. Why *had* Dad gone looking inside our wheelie bin – unless he hadn't completely believed Matthew's story all along?

Suddenly Dad yelled up the stairs again, sounding angrier this time, 'Matthew! Esmie! Get down here, *now*!'

'He must have found more evidence,' I exclaimed. 'What else have you and Jake left lying about, Matthew?'

'Nothing,' Matty said, but he sounded pretty worried.

When we got downstairs, Dad was standing in the hall holding a letter in his hand, looking stern. (Lizzie was still in the kitchen, keeping out of the way – which is always a bad sign.)

'I just found *this* lying on the doormat,' Dad said, handing the letter to us to read together.

DEAR MR HARVEY

I AM WRITING TO LET YOU KNOW THAT IT WAS YOUR SON, MATTHEW, WHO VANDALIZED YOUR NEIGHBOUR'S CAR. I ALSO KNOW THAT HE RECENTLY

VANDALIZED THE SCHOOL SIGN AND BROKE THE SCHOOL FENCE. IF YOU DON'T BELIEVE ME ASK YOUR DAUGHTER . . .

It was printed in capital letters on plain white paper and it wasn't signed.

I looked at my brother in dismay. '*This* must be what Ian meant when he said to expect trouble. He must have come back and posted this through our letter box just now. Jake must have told him everything.'

'Shut up, Esmie,' Matthew snapped, and I realized at once what I'd done.

'So it's true then, is it?' Dad said, fixing his gaze on me.

'Well . . . no . . .' I flushed. 'I reckon . . . I reckon this is what detectives call a poison-pen letter . . . and you really shouldn't believe anything this sort of letter says, should you, Dad?'

Dad gave me a half-amused kind of look. 'And what's your theory about why this letter mentions *you* then?'

'Esmie hasn't got anything to do with this, Dad,' Matthew butted in quickly.

Our father turned to face him. 'OK, so *you* tell me what this is all about then. And if you lie to me again, you're going to be sorry. Understand?'

Matthew bit his lip. 'Jake and me thought it would be a good joke to paint the school sign, that's all. But we had to stand on the fence to reach it and it broke. That's how I fell and got that splinter.'

'They changed Mr Thackery and Miss Dumont's names to *Mr Thick* and *Miss Dumb*,' I added. 'It was really funny, Dad – everyone thought so.'

'Except Mr Thackery and Miss Dumont, I presume?' Dad said drily.

'Well . . .' Matthew flushed.

'So how badly did you damage the fence?' Dad asked.

'The section next to the gate collapsed,' Matty told him, 'but we didn't mean that to happen, Dad. It was an accident.'

'I see. And what about Frank's car? Was that an accident too?'

Matty looked uncomfortable. 'That was . . . that was meant to be a joke because he was complaining about Hercule . . . it was just paw prints, Dad . . . I didn't think about them not coming off . . . I . . . I guess we should have used different paint . . .'

And that's when Dad lost his temper. 'You shouldn't have used ANY paint!' he yelled. '*And* you tried to put the blame on somebody else!'

'Jake did it too,' I piped up. 'It was his idea!'

Dad rounded on me then. 'And why did *you* lie to me earlier, young lady?'

I gulped. 'Well . . .'

'You're grounded for the rest of the day – and as for you, Matthew . . .' He was looking at my brother as if he was having to concentrate all his energy into not giving him a smack. '*You're* grounded until I decide otherwise.'

'But I've got a date with Jennifer tomorrow,' Matthew protested. 'We just arranged it. I can't let her down when we've only just—' He broke off abruptly as Dad looked like he was about to explode. 'Sorry,' he gulped, 'but, please, Dad, if I could just—'

'You can just call her and tell her you won't be seeing her tomorrow – that's what you can just do,' Dad barked. 'God, Matthew, I must have done a really bad job bringing you up, if you think you can do something like this and treat it so lightly.'

'I'm not treating it lightly, Dad. I just—'

'Go to your room! When Jake phones back I'm going to speak to his parents about this. Then I'll decide what to do with you.'

I watched my brother make a hasty exit, before saying meekly, '*I* don't have to go to my room too, do I?'

'You can go and help Lizzie in the kitchen.

But, Esmie, listen to me . . . your brother is in a lot of trouble and I want you to stay out of it, OK?'

I nodded obediently, but, of course, what Dad was forgetting was that I have a *nose* for trouble – and that makes it very difficult for me to stay out of it.

Lizzie was in the kitchen trying to make a cheese-and-bacon quiche and she asked if I wanted to roll out the pastry.

'No thanks,' I replied, slumping down on the nearest seat. Normally I'd have jumped at the chance to do any sort of baking with Lizzie, but right now I had other things on my mind. The business with Matty was bad enough, but I was also worried about Nevada and whether or not I could trust her.

As I watched Lizzie roll out the pastry herself, I decided to ask her what *she* thought about psychics.

'That's a strange question,' she said, sounding surprised. 'I don't think it's the sort of thing children should get involved with, if that's what you mean.'

'Why not?'

'It just isn't.'

'Dad thinks it's just a load of rubbish,' I said.

'A lot of it probably is, Esmie, but I've never had any wish to dabble in it.'

'Is that because it scares you?'

'I suppose it does a bit – yes.'

'Is that because you believe psychics really *can* make contact with the dead?'

'Of course not.'

'Then why do you find it scary?'

'I just do, Esmie, OK?' Lizzie was clearly floundering on the logic front now. (And on the pastry front too, judging by the way it kept breaking up every time she tried to roll it out.)

Dad came into the kitchen to tell us he had spoken to Jake's mother on the phone and he was taking Matthew round to Jake's house. 'After that we're going to see Frank.' He sighed loudly. 'That should be fun.'

'Is Jake going too?' I asked him.

'Yes. Now remember, Esmie,' he told me, 'you're grounded today. Any nonsense and Lizzie will send you straight to your room.'

'OK, Dad,' I said, giving him my most angelic smile.

He was gone by the time the doorbell rang ten minutes later.

'Hello, Nevada,' I heard Lizzie say when she went to answer it. 'Yes, Esmie *is* in, but I'm afraid . . .'

I raced out into the hall before she could

inform Nevada that I was grounded and therefore not allowed to receive visitors.

'It's OK for friends to visit *me*, Lizzie,' I told her, 'just so long as *I* don't visit *them*.' And before Lizzie could question the rules of being grounded (which she isn't totally familiar with yet, thank goodness), I had whisked Nevada up to my room.

12

'There's no message inside,' I told Nevada, trying not to sound too resentful as I handed the jewellery box to her. 'It's completely empty.'

She frowned, taking it from me. 'You've looked really carefully?'

'Of course.'

'Let me try something. But you'll need to close the curtains and stay quiet so I can concentrate.'

She sat on my bed in the darkened room, holding the box on her lap. 'I'll need something else,' she said. 'That photo should do.'

I gave her my mother's picture and she held it in one hand while she touched the lid of the jewellery box with the other. 'I'm going to close my eyes and see if I can conjure up that dream again in my mind.' She screwed up her brow as if she was concentrating really hard and sat like that for several minutes until finally she started to speak in a slow, monotonous voice. 'The box is upside down . . . I'm pressing down on the bottom of it . . . There's something important about the centre . . .' She opened her eyes and said in her normal voice, 'That's all I can see.'

We both sat and looked at the box for a minute or two.

'Go on then,' I finally said. 'Try it.' But I still felt sceptical.

I watched as she turned the box upside down and pressed down firmly on the exact centre of its base – and suddenly there was a clicking sound as if a catch had been released.

My head felt like it was spinning as I watched her lift the bottom right off.

'Look!' she exclaimed. She had found a shallow compartment, inside which was a folded piece of paper. She took it out and handed it to me, looking excited. On the front of the paper, printed in capital letters, were the words *TOP SECRET*.

My hands felt shaky as I took the paper from her and unfolded it. It appeared to be some sort of handwritten document.

MEMBERSHIP CERTIFICATE

This is to certify that Claire Harris is an official member of The Mysterious Four Club

<u>*Members*</u>*: Claire, Kirsten, Amanda, Rusty*
<u>*Our mission*</u>*: To solve mysteries and be best friends forever*
<u>*Our meeting place*</u>*: The Palace Pier*
<u>*Our special date*</u>*: 21st November*
<u>*Our secret sign*</u>*: Holding a whirly ice cream*
<u>*Our secret password*</u>*: ESMERELDA*

'Is it your mother's?' Nevada asked in a hushed voice.

I nodded. Claire Harris had been my mother's name before she'd got married to my dad. 'Look!' I exclaimed, showing it to her. '*My* name is the secret password!'

I've always known I was named after my mother's aunt, so the password was clearly in honour of *her* rather than me, but still . . .

Nevada held the piece of paper flat on the palms of her hands, as if she was holding some ancient precious parchment that might disintegrate into dust if it wasn't treated with due reverence.

'This is definitely a message to you from your mother,' she declared in an awed voice.

I nodded, only half listening. 'Grandma *said* my mum and her friends had a secret club when she stayed in Brighton, so this must be it.'

'Is the Palace Pier in Brighton then?'

'Yes, but it's not called that any more. It's called Brighton Pier now, because it's the only pier left.' Dad had taken Matty and me to Brighton a number of times, because it only takes a couple of hours to get there from where we live, and he had told us that there used to be two piers in Brighton – the West Pier and the Palace Pier. The West Pier had become derelict years ago and so the remaining pier – which had masses of great rides and other amusements on it – had been renamed.

'There are loads of places to buy whirly ice creams at the seaside,' I went on excitedly, 'so that explains their special sign. But what about their special date?'

'November the twenty-first is next week,' Nevada pointed out.

'I know – but I can't think what's special about it.'

Nevada was looking thoughtful. 'You know, even though your mother didn't *originally* write this as a message for you, there must be some reason why she wants you to find it now.'

I frowned. 'What do you mean?'

'Well, otherwise she wouldn't be using me to guide you to it, would she?'

'Are you saying that my *mother* made you dream about the secret compartment?' I asked in disbelief.

'Your mother's spirit – yes. Think about it, Esmie. We're only a few days away from the special date. That can't be a coincidence.'

I felt a bit shivery. 'This is all really weird.'

'Do you want to stop?' she asked quickly. 'We can stop any time, you know.'

'No, of course not. It's just . . .' I trailed off. Part of me was terrified at the prospect of the mother I had always thought was sadly (but safely) dead, coming back to life in some ghost-like form. But on the other hand I had longed to meet her for so long . . . 'I suppose I could phone my grandma and ask her if *she* knows what the date means,' I offered.

'There's no need,' Nevada said quickly. 'I'll be able to work out what your mum's trying to tell you, as long as I spend some more time with you. I'll call in for you on the way to school tomorrow, OK?' As I nodded she added, 'By the way, you mustn't tell anyone else about this – especially not Holly.'

'Why?' I asked. 'Holly won't tell anyone else if I make her promise not to, and she's really good at working out puzzles and riddles and stuff.' I really wanted to tell Holly about my mother's message – not least because I was sure my news would make her forget all about falling out with me.

'The spirit world doesn't like being gossiped about,' Nevada said firmly. 'They might stop sending us messages if we don't keep this just between the two of us. Anyway, Holly will make fun of everything.'

'No she won't. She'll—'

'If you tell her, then I'm not helping you any more, OK?'

So I knew I had no choice but to drop the subject of Holly.

But there was still my grandma in Chicago, and after Nevada had gone I decided to call her. It would be quite early in the morning there, but not so early that I'd wake my grandmother up.

I crept into Dad's bedroom to use the phone where Lizzie wouldn't hear me.

'Esmie!' Grandma exclaimed when she heard my voice. 'Is everything all right?'

'It's fine, Grandma. It's just a quick call this time because I need to ask you something. It's about that club you told me my mum belonged to in Brighton. Was it called the *Mysterious* Four Club?'

'That was it! How did you find out?'

'And did they use the Palace Pier as their meeting place?'

'That's right. They'd hold their meetings right at the very end of it, no matter what the weather was like.'

'And did my mother eat a lot of whirly ice creams?'

'She certainly did! She liked ones with strawberry sauce on top.'

'And was there anything special about November the twenty-first?' I crossed my fingers for luck as I asked that.

'How do you mean?' Grandma sounded puzzled now.

'Well, did anything happen on that date that would have been special to my mum or to the Mysterious Four Club?'

'What a strange question! I can't think of anything. We always went to Brighton in the summer, not in November. Oh . . . but wait a minute . . . the very first time we went there *was* in November – it must have been, because it was just after Esmerelda bought the place, and she had us all down there for a big birthday party. Her birthday was in November, you see – but the eighth, not the twenty-first. That was the year she was forty.' Grandma sighed. 'Esmerelda died young like your mother, I'm afraid. She was only forty-nine.'

'That's not *that* young,' I pointed out.

Grandma let out an indignant snort. 'How dare you, young lady! Now what's all this about?'

'I found my mum's membership certificate for the Mysterious Four Club,' I explained. 'It was with her things that were in the attic.' I decided it was safest not to tell my grandmother about the secret compartment in the jewellery box or about Nevada's psychic predictions.

'Really? She must have kept it an awfully long time. You must show me when I see you at Christmas. Now, where's your father? I wouldn't mind a quick word with him.'

'He's out with Matty,' I said. 'Matty's in trouble again and Dad's probably going to ground him for the rest of his life.' I didn't add that I was temporarily grounded too. 'I'd better go now, Grandma.'

We said our goodbyes and as I came off the phone, I thought about how the twenty-first of November was less than a week away. And I still had no idea what was so special about it.

❧ 13 ❧

When Dad and Matthew eventually came
home, my brother was looking miserable.

'But the school sign was just a prank, Dad,'
Matty was saying as they came in the door.
'Even Jake's dad thought *that* was funny. Surely
we don't have to tell the school it was us. I
mean, what if we get suspended? I'll do really
badly in my exams if I miss too many classes.'

'You should have thought about that sooner
then, shouldn't you?' Dad retorted. 'Prank or
no prank, you still destroyed school property,
which is why we're going to speak to Mr
Thackery tomorrow.'

They had just been to see Mr Stevens, and
apparently our dad and Jake's dad had agreed
to pay for the damage to his car. Matty and Jake
were going to pay *them* back over the next few
months – which in Matty's case meant giving
up the money he had saved from his summer
job, having his allowance cut right back and

washing Dad's car every week until the debt was paid off. Dad had also volunteered Matty to wash Mr Stevens's car every week for free, but luckily for my brother Mr Stevens had declined, saying that he didn't trust anyone else to clean his car the way he liked it.

'Is Mr Stevens going to tell the police?' I asked anxiously. 'Is Matty going to get arrested?'

'I'm going to take Matthew and Jake down to the police station myself tonight,' Dad said. 'They'll get a talking-to, but I don't think they'll get arrested.'

'Can't *you* just give them a talking-to, Dad?' I asked. 'Or does it have to be a policeman who's in charge of vandalism rather than murders?'

'Oh, shut up, Esmie,' Matthew grunted.

'OK, Matthew, get upstairs,' Dad told him sternly. 'You can write a letter of apology to Frank and then you can write one to Mr Thackery and Miss Dumont.'

'Jake isn't having to write any letters,' my brother said sulkily.

'Yes, well, if Jake was my son, he would be. Now move it.'

Later that evening while Dad was at the police station with Matty and Jake, and Lizzie was downstairs watching television, I decided to phone Holly. 'I'm sorry I upset you, Holly,' I said, 'but I didn't think you'd mind me telling Nevada you fancied Matty.'

'Of course I mind! I don't go around telling everyone who *you* fancy, do I?'

'No, but that's only because I don't fancy anyone,' I said. 'But I'm sorry, OK?'

'Yeah, well I just don't like being left out of things, that's all,' Holly said sharply.

'How do you mean?' I asked, thinking for a moment that she had somehow found out about my mother's message.

'Just because I wouldn't agree to help get Matthew and Jennifer back together, you went off and got *Nevada* to help you instead.'

'Oh, that!' I immediately saw my opportunity to make things better. 'Holly, you were so right about Matty and Jennifer. We *shouldn't* have interfered.' I filled her in on Matthew's date with Carys – and how it had seemed to work at first, because Jennifer *had* wanted to go out with my brother again. 'But now Ian is really angry and he's put a note through our door telling Dad it was Matty who painted the school sign and our neighbour's car – and Dad's grounded Matty, so he won't be able to see Jennifer again for ages anyhow.'

'Matthew painted a car?'

'Yeah.' I quickly filled her in on that part too, and about how much trouble my brother was in because of it.

'Poor Matty,' Holly said with feeling.

I was about to tell her not to feel too sorry for him, since in my opinion he'd brought most of this on himself, but I decided to keep quiet. Holly can get very defensive about Matty – which just goes to show that love is blind. (And in Holly's case, deaf too, since my brother only ever speaks to her when he's telling her to get lost.)

'Holly, I told Nevada she can walk to school with me tomorrow. You don't mind, do you? She doesn't know anyone here, except me.'

'OK – just as long as she doesn't want to hang out with us all the time *in* school too,' Holly answered grumpily.

I didn't say anything because I was pretty sure that Nevada *would* want to hang out with us for most of the time in school tomorrow. If only I could tell Holly about that message in my mother's jewellery box and how if it wasn't for Nevada I'd never have found it. Then I was sure Holly would like her a bit more. But Nevada had made me promise not to tell Holly anything, and I was too scared to disobey her. After all, *she* was the expert on the spirit world, not me, and if she said the spirits didn't want

Holly to know about it, then who was I to disagree?

When Nevada called in for me the next morning, I could tell at once that she'd been crying.

'What's wrong?' I asked.

'My mum and dad want Carys and me to go and join them in Saudi Arabia. They were supposed to only be going there for a few months, but now Dad thinks his job is really good and Mum says they want to stay. She says she can home-tutor me if I want, or I can go to an English-speaking school there.'

'When would you have to go?' I asked.

'Soon. But Carys says there's no way *she's* moving to Saudi, and my aunt says we can *both* stay here with her and Uncle Frank if we want to. I don't know what to do. If I stay here I won't be living with Mum and Dad any more, but if I go there I won't know anybody again, and Carys won't even be there this time. Dad will probably get a different job after a year or two anyway and we'll have to move on again. I wish we could *all* just stay put for a while so I can live with Mum and Dad *and* make some friends.'

'Well, you've already made one friend here,' I said, trying my best to cheer her up.

She sniffed. 'Really?'

'Of course!'

'But Holly's still your *best* friend, right?'

'Well . . .' I felt sorry for her but I also knew that I couldn't lie about this. 'Holly's been my friend for a really long time – I mean I've known her for nearly my whole life. But I think you and I are really good friends considering we've only just met, don't you?'

She sniffed again. 'I suppose.' She pulled out a tissue to wipe her nose. 'Well, you're *my* best friend in any case.'

I didn't know what to say to that, so we walked along in silence for a bit and she seemed to have cheered up by the time we met Holly at the school gate.

At lunchtime we were all standing in the canteen queue together when Holly suddenly asked me if I wanted to go round to hers after school. I was just about to agree when Nevada announced that she wanted me to go back to *her* house today instead.

'Well, she can't,' Holly said abruptly.

'Esmie, you *need* to,' Nevada said, giving me a meaningful look.

I managed to get Nevada on her own at the sandwich counter while Holly was waiting for her baked potato. 'Look, Holly did ask me first,' I told her.

'I know, but I think I've worked out what your mum is trying to tell you,' she whispered. 'Though I need to see that message again before I can be sure. Look, if you're not interested that's fine, but—'

'No, I *am* interested,' I interrupted her. 'Just let me figure out a way to tell Holly without upsetting her, OK?'

I didn't know what to do until Miss Dumont came to find me in Registration that afternoon and inadvertently took the whole thing out of my hands. She looked quite grave-faced as she walked into our classroom and announced that she wanted a private word with me, and I had a momentary panic that something had happened to Dad. (I'm always imagining he's been killed in a high-speed car chase, or shot by one of his murderers, even though he keeps telling me he hardly ever chases any dangerous criminals in his day-to-day work.)

As soon as Miss Dumont got me out into the corridor she said crisply, 'Your brother is starting a week of detentions today, Esmie. That means there'll be no one at home after school, so your father has arranged with Holly's mum for you to go home with Holly.'

When I went back into the classroom and told Holly (who sits next to me), she was so overjoyed that you'd think I hadn't been round to her house after school in ten years or something.

I had to wait until the bell rang to let Nevada know. 'I'll try and come round to yours after Dad picks me up from Holly's tonight,' I told her apologetically.

'Yeah, well just make sure it isn't too late,' she replied, scowling.

'Nevada, do you *really* think you know what my mum's message means?' I asked, hoping she might give me some sort of sneak preview.

She nodded. 'I had another dream.'

And then Holly joined us and she completely clammed up.

☙ 14 ☙

Holly and I have been friends for so long that her bedroom seems almost as familiar to me as my own. I really love Holly's pink wallpaper and the gold stars she and her mum stencilled on to it, and the fluffy bright pink rug that lies in the middle of her floor. I was really worried she was going to change it last year when she started complaining that pink wasn't a cool colour any more, but fortunately she reverted back to liking it again after I showed her a picture of a famous celebrity's ultra-pink bedroom in *Hello!* magazine.

Right now Holly was lying on her back on the floor and I was lolling on the bed, flicking through a bridal magazine that Holly had bought for me. 'I thought we could choose what dress Lizzie would look best in, and then we could choose you a bridesmaid's dress to match,' she said.

I was touched. Holly knows how desperate

I am for Dad and Lizzie to get married, and she also knows how much I've always dreamed of being a bridesmaid.

'But would Lizzie still be able to wear a proper bride's dress if they get married in a registry office?' I asked doubtfully.

'Of course she would! Anyway, just because it's not a church wedding, it doesn't mean it *has* to be a registry office. They could get married in a posh hotel or stately home – or in a castle in Scotland like celebrities do.'

As we flicked through the pages of the wedding magazine together, stopping to comment on each dress in turn, I thought about how Dad and Lizzie hadn't actually said that they *wanted* to get married.

'I hope they don't decide just to live together,' I said. 'I mean, Dad's already been married once. He might not want to do it again.'

'Yes, but Lizzie hasn't been married before, has she? You should take this magazine home with you and leave it where she can see it. I bet she won't be able to resist the idea of getting married when she sees some of these dresses.'

'Yes, but I think if Dad sees the *cost* of some of these dresses it might put him off.'

'I don't see why. Lizzie can buy her own dress – or her parents can buy it for her. It's traditional for the bride's parents to pay for the wedding.'

'Lizzie's dad is dead and I don't think Lizzie's mum would buy her a dress,' I said. (I've never actually met Lizzie's mother, but according to Lizzie she's quite a difficult person, which is why Lizzie lives at the opposite end of the country from her.)

'I've just had an idea!' Holly exclaimed. 'You know how you told me your mum's old wedding dress is still in a box up in your loft? Well, why doesn't Lizzie wear that? Then it wouldn't cost anything.'

I looked at her.

'OK, maybe not,' she said swiftly. 'Let's look for some cheaper ones in here, shall we? Look, this one's only *three* thousand pounds . . .'

I was having such a great time with Holly that the next hour flew by, and we were laughing so much when her mum came and knocked on her bedroom door that we didn't hear her at first.

'Your dad just phoned, Esmie. He's going to be later than he expected, so he's asked if you can stay for tea.'

'But Matty'll be home by now,' I said, checking my watch. 'I can have tea with him.'

'Apparently your dad just phoned your

house and Matty didn't pick up. He's not answering his mobile either.'

'But Matty's detention finished ages ago –' I began.

'– and he was meant to go straight home afterwards,' Holly's mum finished for me. 'That's what your dad just told me too. He didn't sound very happy.'

'Uh-oh!' I exclaimed. 'Matty's going to be in even *more* trouble now. Where can he have gone?'

'Your dad says he'll come and pick you up on his way back, which should be in an hour or so. I've just put a lasagne in the oven, so you can eat that with us.'

'Did I tell you that Lizzie makes really good lasagne?' I told them. 'And chilli con carne.'

'Yes, you did,' Holly said, yawning loudly. 'About a million times.'

Holly's mum smiled at me. 'Lizzie sounds like a much better cook than me, Esmie. Our lasagne is straight from the supermarket, I'm afraid!'

'Yes, but Lizzie still only knows how to cook three things,' I pointed out (because I was counting the shepherd's pie now as well).

'Maybe she should go on a cookery course before she marries your dad,' Holly said.

'Holly, don't be so sexist!' her mum exclaimed.

'Yes – and it's not like they've actually *decided* to get married,' I added quickly, just in case Holly's mum got the wrong idea and started congratulating Dad on his engagement when he turned up to collect me tonight.

Dad wasn't in a very good mood when he eventually arrived to pick me up, which I guessed was because of my brother.

'Holly's mum said Matty wasn't in when you rang home,' I said as I climbed into the car.

'That's right.'

'Have you tried him again since? He might've just been in the bathroom or something.'

'I tried him several times. The first time he picked up was half an hour ago.'

'Where did he say he'd been?'

'He didn't.'

We fell silent after that and I decided it was best not to question Dad any more. Matthew was in big trouble, but then he was stupid if he thought he could stay out late when he was meant to be grounded, and get away with it. Besides, I had my own problem to solve. I had told Nevada I wouldn't be late home but now I was, and I didn't know how she'd react if I called in on her. I had to see her though, because I really wanted to know whatever it was she had to tell me about my mother.

As we drove into our street I noticed there were several people standing in our neighbour's driveway three houses along. Dad pulled into our drive and, as we both climbed out of the car, we saw that Mr Stevens was standing in the group. He waved to Dad to get his attention and when Dad didn't respond he started to walk towards us.

'Have you seen what your son has done now?' he called out.

Dad turned to look at him. 'Pardon?' Something in his voice made me think that he was starting not to like Mr Stevens very much.

'Come and see this!'

Dad and I followed him to where our other neighbours were gathered. The couple whose drive they were standing in didn't seem to be in the group, but everyone was staring at their van, which they use for their organic fruit and vegetable business.

It was dark, but Mr Stevens had a torch and as Dad approached he pointed it at the side of the van, saying, 'I thought I saw someone out here on the drive, and since Robert and Anne are away I came out to take a look.'

Dad and I stared at the van, which usually

says *Robert's Organic Fruit & Veg* on the side in big red letters. But now the word Robert had been altered so that the round bit of the letter 'b' had been painted out along with the 't' and the 's', and what was left of it had been added to with red paint, so the whole thing now read *Rotten Organic Fruit & Veg*.

I started to giggle. I couldn't help it.

'Esmie, go home now,' Dad said sharply.

I didn't argue with him. I could tell he was putting two and two together – the fact that Matthew had been out when he'd phoned, and now this.

I hurried back to our own house and let myself in with my key. To my surprise, Lizzie was there. 'I thought you were going out tonight,' I said.

'I got back twenty minutes ago. Where's your dad?'

'He's just coming. Where's Matty?'

'Upstairs.'

I ran up the stairs and burst into my brother's room without even knocking. 'Matty, Dad knows what you did! You are in *so* much trouble!'

My brother was lying on his front on the bed with a geography textbook open in front of him. 'How can he know already?' he asked in dismay.

'Mr Stevens just showed him the van. Half the street's out there looking at it!'

'*What* van?'

'The van you just painted of course! Did Jake help you?'

'We haven't painted any van! Esmie, what are you talking about?'

'Don't be stupid, Matty. It's obvious it was you, and anyway, Dad phoned you loads of times after school and you were out.'

'I was round at Jennifer's!'

'Jennifer's?'

'Yes. I thought that's what you were talking about. I know I'm meant to be grounded and that Dad thinks I cancelled my date with her . . . but I have to keep seeing her, or Ian's going to move in on her again.'

'But Matty . . .' I was really confused now. 'What about the van?'

'*What* van?' he asked again, sounding really impatient this time.

Just then we heard the front door slamming and Dad's voice yelling up the stairs. 'MATTHEW! WHERE ARE YOU?'

I looked at my brother. 'The fruit-and-veg van. Do you *really* not know about it?'

Matthew shook his head, starting to look pale. 'Look, whatever happens, don't tell him I was with Jennifer.'

'But, Matty—'

'Just promise me you won't interfere this time, Esmie. *Please.*'

I sighed. 'All right then – but it's your funeral.'

15

I knew I had no chance of asking Dad if I could go round to see Nevada after that, because it was as if our house had suddenly become a major war zone. And since everyone knows that innocent people get killed in wars, I picked up Hercule (who was sitting very unwisely at the top of the stairs) and went to take cover in my bedroom – keeping the door open so I could still hear everything.

As soon as Dad flung open Matthew's door, the yelling started.

'I didn't do it, Dad!' my brother kept saying.

'Don't give me that, Matthew! It's exactly the same thing that you and Jake did before! Was Jake involved with this as well?'

'No! It wasn't us!'

'So where were you when I phoned? You were meant to come straight home after detention.'

'I know. I'm sorry.' My brother sounded like

he was close to tears – he acts all tough half the time, but he isn't really – not underneath.

'You *will* be sorry. This isn't funny, Matthew. It's vandalism, and if you think you're going to get away with it then you're wrong.'

There was a load more shouting and then Dad started to empty Matty's room of his Game Boy, his computer, his music system and his television set, all of which he carried out on to the landing. 'These are all going into the garage, and you can stay in your room until I decide what else to do with you!'

He slammed Matty's door when he was finished, and swore as he stubbed his toe on the edge of the TV set on his way to the stairs.

I waited until he'd gone, then I quietly opened Matthew's door and went inside. My brother was standing at the window and his eyes were wet with tears, which he rubbed away roughly when he saw me.

'What do *you* want?' he hissed.

'To help you.' I looked round his room, which, without all the gadgets Dad had confiscated, looked very empty all of a sudden.

'Dad *hates* me!' Matty burst out.

'No he doesn't!' I went over and sat down on the bed. 'I think he probably wants to make your room look like the sort of room you'd have in prison, to show you what it would be like there. Because you might end up in prison, if you keep spray-painting all our neighbours' cars.'

'I only painted *one* car. I told Dad I wouldn't do it again and I haven't. I honestly haven't, Esmie.'

'Well if *you* didn't do it, who did?'

'I don't know.' Matty sniffed. 'But it wasn't me!'

I really wanted to believe him. The trouble was, considering what had happened previously, there was no doubt that my brother and Jake had to be the prime suspects. Unless . . .

'Do you think Ian might have done it?' I asked. 'To get you into more trouble, I mean?'

Matthew started to shake his head, then stopped. 'Ian rang Jennifer while I was there today. She wanted to get rid of him, so she told him I was with her. Do you think that could've made him even more jealous?'

I scrambled to my feet. 'We've got to tell Dad.'

'No!' Matty looked alarmed. 'We can't tell him where I was.'

'But Matty, Jennifer's your only alibi.'

'If Dad finds out, he'll phone up Jennifer's dad and he might stop her from seeing me again.'

'What difference does it make? Dad's going

to ground you for ever after this, so you won't get to see her anyway.' (Jennifer goes to a different school from us, which meant Matty wouldn't be able to see her during the day either.)

'She's promised to come and meet me every day after detention and walk home with me, so we *will* still get to see each other,' Matthew said. 'Unless her dad finds out and stops her.' He sighed. 'Look, there must be some other way of convincing Dad that I didn't paint that van. *You're* really good at making stuff up, Esmie. Can't *you* figure out something to tell him that he'll believe?'

I stared at my brother. This was the first time he had ever openly asked for my help, and I had to admit I was touched.

'I'll see what I can do,' I said. 'But I'm not promising anything.'

'Thanks, Ez. Look, I'd better get on with my homework.'

I left his room, carefully stepping round all the stuff on the landing, which Hercule was now sniffing suspiciously. If I could just sow a seed of doubt in Dad's mind about Matty, I thought . . .

When I got downstairs, I could hear Dad and Lizzie having a heated conversation in the kitchen.

Lizzie sounded upset. 'Well, something must have triggered it and I don't see what else it could be!'

'But he hasn't *said* that he's unhappy about that, has he?'

'No, but what if this is his way of saying it! Look, John, you just said yourself that it's a mystery why he's behaving like this. Well, what if he just can't handle me moving in with you? I mean, how do you know *what* he's thinking? You never talk to him.'

'I talk to him all the time!'

'I mean you never talk to him about *us*.'

'Yes, well, as far as I'm concerned, he doesn't get to destroy other people's property, full stop,' Dad snapped. 'No matter *how* he feels about you becoming his stepmother!'

I had been about to burst into the kitchen to tell Lizzie that Matthew's behaviour had nothing to do with her, but at that point I got a bit sidetracked. Instead I burst in exclaiming, '*Is* Lizzie going to be our stepmum? When are you and her getting married, Dad? Can I be the bridesmaid?'

Lizzie jumped as if I'd given her a terrible fright, and Dad stared at me as if I was some sort of horrible apparition with two heads, rather than his daughter.

'You really should stop listening outside

doors, Esmie,' he said crossly. 'I was just illustrating a point about Matthew, that's all. Now scram!'

'You're wrong about Matty painting that van, Dad. He says he didn't do it and I believe him. *I* think it was Ian. He's got a motive too, you know!'

'What motive?' Dad demanded.

'Ian wants to get Matty grounded for as long as possible, so Jennifer will get fed up with waiting for him and dump him again.' When Dad didn't look particularly convinced, I added, 'After all, nobody actually saw Matty paint that van, did they? So it could just as easily have been Ian.'

'Except that Matthew won't tell me where he was after school,' Dad retorted sharply, 'which means he's clearly got something to hide. Now leave us alone, please, Esmie. Lizzie and I are talking.'

I suddenly remembered that I still had my own problem to sort out, and my instincts told me that now might be a good time to take advantage of Dad's obvious desire to see the back of me. 'Dad, can I go across the road and see Nevada?' I asked quickly. 'There's something I need to speak to her about.'

He looked at the kitchen clock and I could

tell he was tempted, but he still shook his head. 'It's too late to be going out now, Esmie.'

'But it's important, Dad. It's . . . it's to do with school. I need to check something about my homework.'

'Well, why don't you ring her?'

'I don't know her number.'

'Well, try looking it up in the phone book under Stevens.'

So I ended up calling Nevada from the phone in Dad's room. Her aunt answered and when Nevada came to the phone she sounded very unfriendly. 'Yes?'

'Look, I'm really sorry I couldn't come round,' I told her, 'but my dad didn't pick me up from Holly's house until really late, and then there's been loads of trouble with Matthew—'

'I know about Matthew. Uncle Frank's been going on about it all night. Your brother's really stupid if you ask me.'

'Well, he says he didn't do it and I believe him, but –' I broke off abruptly. 'Nevada, what was it you were going to tell me about my mum? You said you had another dream.'

'Oh, that . . .' She let out an impatient sigh. 'Look I don't really have anything else to tell you. I just *said* I'd had another dream, because

I really wanted you to come round to mine instead of Holly's after school. I guess it didn't work though, did it?'

And she cut me off before I could reply.

◖ 16 ◗

Nevada didn't call in for me on her way to school the next morning, so I could only assume she was still in a major huff with me, despite the fact that I was the one who now had more reason to be cross with *her*. But the strange thing was that, instead of feeling angry with Nevada for lying to me about my mother, I actually felt quite relieved. It wasn't that I had stopped feeling excited about the message hidden inside my mother's jewellery box. It was just that I was starting to think that maybe Nevada's psychic powers had gone as far as I wanted them to. After all, if she was actually capable of bringing my mother's spirit even closer, it would not only be an incredibly big deal, but . . . let's face it . . . an incredibly *scary* one.

I met Holly as I approached the school gate. 'You'll never guess what's happened,' I exclaimed as I greeted her. I started to explain about how Matty was being blamed for painting our neighbour's van even though I was almost positive he was innocent. 'The trouble is, Matty won't tell Dad where he was at the time the crime was committed,' I told Holly, 'which means he's got no alibi.' Of course, when I told her where Matty had really been, Holly was all for telling Dad the truth at once – even if that meant Matty wasn't going to be able to see Jennifer again for ages. But I had another idea. 'I'm going to find out who really did it and make them confess,' I told her.

'How are you going to do that?'

'I'm going to treat this like a proper criminal investigation. Dad isn't doing that, see, which is why he's already accused the wrong person. First I'm going to check out the crime scene, then I'm going to interview Ian, since he's my chief suspect.' I paused. 'I don't suppose you want to help, do you?'

Holly grinned. 'Of course! Anything to help Matthew!'

'That's great. Let's start today after school.'

I immediately felt heaps better, and when I spotted Nevada on her own in the playground, waiting for the bell to ring, I felt a surge of friendliness towards her.

Without consulting Holly, I went over to speak to her. 'Nevada, you know how you said that when you grow up you want to be the sort of psychic who helps detectives with their investigations?'

'Yeah. So?' She gave me a wary look, as if she was trying to decide if I was making fun of her or not.

'Well, there's something that Holly and I really need your help with – it's to do with my brother.' I told her what I had just told Holly – although she knew most of it anyway, since her uncle was one of Matty's chief accusers. Then I told her my plan to expose the person who had *really* painted the van.

'But Matthew actually *admitted* he painted my uncle's car,' Nevada said.

'I know. It's just that he didn't do *this*, even though it looks like it must be the same person. You see, I reckon this is what's called a *copycat* crime.' And I went on to outline my theory that the person who had done *this* crime was trying to set my brother up.

'OK . . .' Nevada began slowly. 'If you say so . . . But how do you want me to help?'

'You sensed all that stuff when I showed you my mum's jewellery box, didn't you? So maybe if we show you the crime scene you might sense something useful *there*.'

Holly had joined us and she was staring at us as if we were both nuts. '*What* did Nevada

sense about your mum's jewellery box, Esmie?'
she wanted to know.

Nevada glared at me threateningly.

'Oh . . . well . . . she sort of guessed . . . well
sensed . . . what was inside it,' I mumbled.

'And what *was* inside it?'

'Jewellery,' Nevada replied before I could
speak.

'Right. So that was really difficult then,'
Holly said sarcastically.

'It was pretty cool actually,' I put in hastily.
'Which is why I've asked her to help us now.
She's going to come to the crime scene with us
and see if she can get any psychic vibes off the
fruit-and-veg van.'

'Yeah . . . right,' Holly said.

'We'll look for fingerprints as well,' I added.
'And other evidence. After school we can pick
up my Crime-Buster Kit and get started.'

'What's your *Crime-Buster Kit*?' Nevada
looked interested now.

I started to tell her what was in it, and when
I got to explaining about the stick of chalk,
Holly began to snigger.

'What's so funny?' I demanded.

'Well, you always say that about it – that
you're meant to use it to draw round dead
bodies – but I reckon it's only in those detective programmes on TV that they do that!'

'No it's not!' I protested. 'That *is* what you're meant to use it for. It shows you in my detective-in-training pocket book.'

To my surprise, Nevada started to giggle then too. 'I know! We could use the chalk to draw round the van!'

Holly laughed even more at that, and for the first time she actually seemed to forget that she didn't like Nevada. 'Esmie's mad about all this detective stuff,' she told her in a confidential tone. 'Did she tell you about the time she borrowed my mum's blonde wig and sunglasses to wear as a disguise, so she could tail Lizzie?'

'Shut up, Holly,' I snapped, because that story is way too embarrassing to have repeated.

Still, I thought, at least she and Nevada finally seemed to be getting on well enough to share a joke with each other – even if it *was* at my expense.

After school Holly and I both rang our parents and got permission to go back to Nevada's house. When we got there, Nevada told her aunt we were going outside for a bit and, as soon as we'd dumped our school bags in the hall, we headed out again. Nevada and Holly waited on the pavement while I let myself into my house to fetch my Crime-Buster Kit from my room – plus a couple of torches because it was already getting dark outside.

The fruit-and-veg van was still parked on its driveway, and luckily nobody else was around as we approached it.

'So what do you want us to do exactly?' Holly asked as I handed her a torch and shone my own on to the side of the van where the letters had been changed.

'Look for evidence,' I said.

Holly moved closer to examine the paint. 'You can see the brush strokes. I wonder whether we can use them to tell whether the culprit was right- or left-handed.'

'There can't be any brush strokes,' I told her. 'It's spray-paint.'

'No it's not. Look.'

So I got out my magnifying glass, shone my own torch closer and inspected the paint that had been added. Holly was right. If you looked closely there were definitely brush strokes. 'This hasn't been spray-painted at all!' I exclaimed.

'Told you so,' Holly said.

'Yes, but don't you see? It's a different MO so this means it's pointing away from Matty and Jake being the ones who did it.' When both Holly and Nevada looked blank, I explained, 'MO stands for modus operandi. It's Latin or something. Anyway it's the term detectives use to describe a criminal's way of working.'

'How do you mean?' Nevada asked.

'Well, say lots of murder victims were all found drowned in the bath with safety pins in their noses, but the last body was found in a swimming pool with no safety pin, well that would be a different MO and it would mean that the last murder was probably committed by someone else.'

'You think up really gory things, Esmie,' Nevada said.

While I was talking, Holly (who's used to my gory stories) was licking her finger and rubbing at the red paint on the van.

'Be careful, Holly,' I warned her. 'We've still got to check for fingerprints, remember.'

'Don't you have to have some sort of special equipment for that?' Nevada asked.

'It says in my crime-busters book that you can use dusting powder or tape,' I told her.

'Give me your keys and I'll go and get some Sellotape,' Holly offered. 'I know where it is. I'll get some talcum powder from the bathroom as well.'

'Thanks, Holly.' As she left, I turned to Nevada. 'If you concentrated really hard like you did with my mum's jewellery box . . . do you think you might get some kind of psychic vibe about the person who did this?'

Nevada looked doubtful. 'I don't know.'

'You can touch the paint if it helps . . . we can always take *your* fingerprints afterwards, to exclude them.'

'Well, I can try . . . but I'm not doing it in front of Holly.'

'Do it now then – while she's gone.'

So Nevada placed one hand, palm-down, over the lettering on the van and closed her eyes. After a minute or two she looked at me again and said, 'I'm getting a really strong feeling that the person who did this doesn't want to be found.'

I sighed. 'I guess that figures. You didn't get any sense about the colour of their hair, did you?'

Nevada shook her head, looking uncomfortable as she stepped away from the van.

A few minutes later Holly came back, holding a roll of Sellotape and the tin of talc I'd given Dad last Christmas. She handed the Sellotape to me and kept hold of the talc. 'So what do we do? Just sprinkle the powder over the side of the van or what?'

I frowned. In the last TV programme I had seen where the detectives had dusted for fingerprints, I was sure they'd used what

162

looked like a big make-up brush to apply the powder. Lizzie had a brush like that which she kept in her make-up bag in the bathroom, but before I could say anything, Holly had prised the lid off the talc and was chucking the whole lot at the van's side.

Suddenly a car pulled up at the end of the driveway and to my horror I saw that it was Dad. He must have come home early to check up on Matty or something. He didn't even park properly before opening his door and striding over to me with a face like thunder. 'Don't tell me *you're* turning into a vandal too, young lady!'

'No, Dad, of course not!' I exclaimed. 'We're just dusting the van for fingerprints. I know Matty and Jake didn't do this, so I'm trying to prove it.'

'That's right,' Holly backed me up firmly. 'And it can't be them because it's a different MO.'

'Look at this, Dad,' I explained quickly. 'This isn't even the same sort of paint Matty used before. *This* was painted on with a brush.' I shone my torch directly on to the side of the van so Dad could see what I meant, but there was so much talc there that it was difficult.

He used his hand to rub off some of the powder. (I guessed I might as well forget about getting any fingerprints after this). 'You're right,' he said after a moment or two. He sounded surprised. 'I didn't look that closely yesterday. None of us did. It was dark and I just assumed it was the same paint.'

'A good detective must never just assume things, Dad,' I reminded him.

He let out a snort. 'Yes, well, apparently I don't always think as much like a detective as you do, Esmie.'

'Shall we see if it washes off?' Holly asked.

'If it's emulsion it should just come off with water,' Dad said. 'Otherwise I've got some white spirit in the garage that might do it. But we'll have to be careful.'

Dad sent the three of us into the house to fetch a bucket of water while he went to find the white spirit, and after we'd been waiting outside with the water for a good five minutes, I decided to go and see what was holding him up.

I found him at the far end of the garage with the light on, staring at something on the floor. I got the feeling he'd been standing there for a while.

I walked inside and as I got closer I saw that he was looking at a small tin of red paint, next to which was a paintbrush. The brush had dried red paint on its bristles.

I gasped. 'Is that . . . ?'

Dad nodded. His voice was strangely tense and quiet as he said, 'At least it's emulsion. I suppose that's something.' He looked at his watch. 'Detention should be finished soon. I think I'll go and meet Matthew from school.'

'Are you *sure* it's the same paint that was used on the van, Dad?' I asked.

'It looks like it to me,' he said.

'Yes, but couldn't you take a paint sample off the van to make sure?'

Dad looked faintly amused. 'Send it in for forensic testing you mean? I don't think that's a particularly good use of police resources do you, Esmie?' He sighed loudly. 'Listen, it's time you girls stopped messing about out there. Matthew can wash the van when he gets back.'

I felt puzzled as I headed back to where Holly and Nevada were waiting. I couldn't believe my brother would lie to me like that. I had been *so* certain Matty was innocent and that Ian had set him up. Unless . . . And that's when I had a sudden thought about the pot of paint in the garage.

The thing was, our garage door had been open for ages the previous evening, because Dad had made several trips to and fro, putting Matty's TV and other stuff inside. Ian could easily have planted that paint pot then – and because he had placed it at the very back of the garage, Dad wouldn't have noticed it when he'd finally locked up. And if I was right, then both the pot and the brush would have Ian's fingerprints on them, rather than Matthew's.

I rushed back into the garage to find Dad holding the paint pot in one hand and the brush in the other. 'Dad, why aren't you wearing gloves?' I wailed. 'You're destroying all the evidence!'

Dad looked at me as if he didn't have a clue what I was on about. 'What evidence?' he asked.

I mean, honestly, at times like these it's hard to believe that my dad is a *real* detective.

🐾 17 🐾

Lizzie arrived home just as Dad was about to go and meet Matty, and since it was just going to be the two of us in the house for the next fifteen minutes, I decided now was a good time to bring out the bridal magazine Holly had given me. I went up to my room to fetch it and placed it in the centre of the coffee table in the living room, where Lizzie couldn't fail to see it. Maybe if I just left it there for her to find herself she would feel less pressured, and more inclined to look at it, than if I actually gave it to her directly.

I switched on the television and waited for her to join me, but unfortunately she took ages doing loads of stuff in the kitchen first. By the time she came into the room, Hercule, who had been sitting in the middle of the floor washing himself, had jumped up on to the coffee table and sat himself down right on top of the picture of the bride.

'Esmie, have you finished your homework?' Lizzie asked, sitting down beside me on the sofa. 'You know you're not meant to watch TV unless you have.'

'I'll do it in a minute!' I gave Hercule a shove, but that just made him dig in his claws so that he slid off the table taking the magazine with him.

'Careful, Esmie. He'll make scratch marks!' Lizzie exclaimed, staying put to inspect the table, rather than going to rescue the magazine from Hercule, who was now lying on his side and subjecting it to a frenzied kicking with his back feet.

Just then the front door opened and Dad came in, followed by Matty. My brother didn't go straight to his room, but went into the kitchen with Dad. Our father seemed a lot calmer than I'd expected, and Matty didn't look nearly as upset either, so I guessed they must have come to some sort of truce in the car. I suddenly remembered that Jennifer had been going to meet Matty after school, and I wondered if Dad had seen her there.

Lizzie went to join them, so I picked up the magazine and put it in her bag, which was underneath the coffee table. She couldn't fail to see it there as the top half was sticking right out. Then I went through to the kitchen too.

Matty was rummaging around under the sink, asking if we had any spare cloths, so I guessed he was about to go and wash the van.

'We left a bucket of water out there for you, Matty,' I told him.

'Matthew *still* claims he had nothing to do with this,' Dad said to Lizzie. 'Even though I've told him I found that paint pot in the garage.'

'Don't you think I'd have hidden it in a less obvious place if I really *had* done it?' Matthew said grumpily.

'Oh, you mean like where you hid that spray-paint can?'

My brother pulled a face, but not so that Dad could see him.

'And change out of your school uniform before you go out there,' Dad added firmly. (Whenever Matty's done something wrong Dad always reverts to treating him like he's about five.)

After my brother had gone upstairs to get changed, Dad said to Lizzie, 'I know it's still inexcusable behaviour, but thank God he's used paint that washes off this time.'

'It wasn't *him*, Dad,' I butted in. 'And if you'd let me finish my investigation then I'd be able to prove it.'

'I don't think we need any further examination of Robert's van, thanks all the same,

Esmie,' Dad said. 'Oh – and did *you* know Matthew was planning to meet Jennifer after school today?' He didn't wait for a reply, but told Lizzie, 'Apparently they were going to walk home together. As Matthew pointed out rather hysterically in the car, if they don't get to do that, then they won't get to see each other for the whole time he's grounded.'

'So what did you tell him?' Lizzie asked.

'I said they could walk home together from tomorrow, as long as they don't take too long about it and we don't get any more painting incidents.'

'Well, that's fair,' Lizzie said, sounding relieved.

'Yes – I must be getting soft in my old age.'

They carried on talking, and I thought what a good influence Lizzie was having on Dad, and how he must have taken in what she'd said about Matthew finding it really difficult to cope with not seeing Jennifer.

I had made myself some toast and was just spreading peanut butter on it, when Matty came downstairs and shouted from the hall that he was going out to wash the van.

As soon as he'd shut the front door behind him Lizzie said, 'Esmie, I really think you should make a start on your homework.'

She obviously wanted to talk to Dad in

private, so I pretended to take my toast up to my room, though instead I doubled back and stood in the hall, listening to what they were saying.

'So did you manage to have a proper talk with him in the car?' Lizzie was asking.

'I tried. He says he isn't worried about you moving in, and that the only thing he's worried about is how he's going to see Jennifer while he's grounded. I told him he should have thought of that *before* he vandalized our neighbour's van, and then he started getting all indignant, insisting he knows nothing about it. The school sign and Frank's car, yes – but not Robert's van.'

'But that's so strange,' Lizzie said. 'I mean, why wouldn't he just admit to that as well? He agreed to wash the van readily enough, didn't he?'

'Well, I think he knew he had no choice as far as that was concerned.'

'At least you were able to talk to him, I suppose.'

'Yes, and you know, Lizzie, although I still don't fully understand what's going on with him, I *really* don't think it has anything to do with you.'

She sighed. 'I hope not.'

'Come on. Let's go and sit down. Do you feel like a glass of wine?'

I suddenly realized they were moving out of the kitchen, so I dived into the hall toilet, which we hardly ever use because it's the size of a broom cupboard, but which provides useful cover whenever I want to eavesdrop. I stayed there until they'd gone into the living room and then I slipped out, but just as I was starting to climb the stairs I heard Dad exclaim, 'What's this?!'

I rushed back to listen at the door and I soon realized he had discovered Holly's bridal magazine.

'Let me see that,' Lizzie said, sounding surprised.

There was a long silence and I kept my fingers crossed that they were both being totally captivated by the beautiful wedding gown on the front cover.

But Dad didn't say anything else until Lizzie asked in a confused voice, 'What is it? Why are you looking at me like that?'

'It's just . . . well . . .' Dad sounded irritated. 'It's just that one minute you're worried Matthew might be twitchy just because you're moving in with us, and the next you're leaving *wedding* magazines lying around the place.'

'This isn't *mine*, John,' Lizzie retorted. 'And if you ask me, *you're* the one who's twitchy.'

Dad sounded impatient. 'Look, you don't have to lie about it, OK?'

'I'm *not* lying.' Lizzie sounded like she was getting cross now.

Dad didn't answer, but I could guess only too well the sort of look he was giving her. It's the one he always gives me and Matty when he thinks we're not being truthful – which I've always imagined is exactly the same look he gives his murder suspects when he interviews *them*.

Clearly I was right, because all of a sudden Lizzie snapped, 'Don't look at me like that, John! And don't you *dare* accuse me of lying. This isn't mine – and even if it was, I don't expect to be interrogated about it!'

'*Interrogated?*'

'Yes! Here you are. Maybe you want to check it for fingerprints.' And she must have thrown the magazine at him, because there was the sound of a thud and a flutter of pages as it landed.

I heard Lizzie walking towards the door and I quickly dived into the kitchen.

'Well, if you didn't put it there, who *did*?' Dad was shouting after her as she headed for the stairs.

'Take a wild guess!' she yelled back.

And it only took another ten seconds after that before Dad was bellowing, 'ESMIE!' at the top of his voice.

When I stepped out into the hall I found Dad standing at the bottom of the stairs holding the magazine – which was now very crumpled. He whirled round when he heard me, looking surprised that I had come from the kitchen. 'Esmie, did *you* put this in Lizzie's bag?' he asked me.

'Well . . . umm . . . sort of . . . yes . . .' I admitted.

'*Why?*'

'I . . . well . . . I just thought she might like looking at the brides' dresses. I didn't mean to make you and Lizzie have a row, Dad. I just thought—'

'I know what you thought, Esmie,' he interrupted, but less sharply this time. He sighed. 'Look, just go upstairs and do your homework, please.'

Reluctantly I did as I was told and I had just reached the top of the stairs when I met Lizzie on the landing. She was carrying her overnight bag and she looked upset.

'Where are you going?' I asked her anxiously.

'I'm going back to my own place for a couple of nights, Esmie.'

'But—'

'Didn't your dad just say you had to do your homework?' she reminded me.

I stayed where I was while she went downstairs. Dad was waiting for her in the hall and she spoke to him calmly. 'I think we both need a bit of space tonight, John.'

'Look, I'm sorry—'

'I need some time to think about things. And I think the children need to spend some time alone with you.'

No, we don't, I felt like shouting down the stairs to her. But I knew she was thinking more about Matthew than about me, so any protestations on my part would be pointless unless Matthew backed them up.

'Lizzie, wait . . .' Dad was following her through the front door now, and I felt my stomach lurch as if I might be sick.

I raced downstairs and watched through the kitchen window as they talked together out at the car. But even though they talked for quite a long time Lizzie still didn't come back inside with him.

'Dad, I'm sorry!' I cried as he returned to the house. 'This is all my fault!'

'No, it's not, Esmie. Grown-ups have rows

sometimes and they need time to cool off, that's all.'

'Dad, Lizzie isn't going to dump us now, is she?' I realized how weird that must sound, since Lizzie was going out with Dad, not me and Matthew, but I didn't care. Lizzie was a big part of *my* life now, as well as Dad's, and I reckoned I needed her just as much as he did. And I reckoned Matty did too, despite all his protests.

Suddenly the front door opened again and we both turned towards it hopefully. But it wasn't Lizzie – it was my brother. He was carrying a bucket of dirty water and the sleeves of his jacket were soaking wet. 'What's going on?' he asked. 'Why did Lizzie drive away just now? I thought she was staying tonight.'

'She's gone back to her own flat,' I told him. 'You were right about her needing to keep it in case she got fed up living with us!' And I let out a loud sob and rushed upstairs to phone Holly.

18

Luckily Holly knows that if there's one thing guaranteed to cheer me up and take my mind off my troubles, it's a piece of detective work.

'Lizzie's obviously upset for two reasons,' she said when I told her what had happened. 'Firstly she thinks that Matty's turning to crime because he can't face having her as his step-mother, and secondly she secretly wants to get married but your dad doesn't. So if we prove that Matty isn't a criminal *and* we get your dad to propose, then everything will be all right, won't it?'

'I don't see how we can make Dad propose,' I said gloomily. 'I've tried everything I can think of.'

'Tell you what – let's start with the other thing,' Holly suggested. 'Let's start by proving Matty didn't paint that fruit-and-veg van.' She paused. 'And if you like we can ask Nevada if she wants to help us.'

I sniffed. 'Thanks, Holly.'

'Yeah, well . . . three heads are better than one, I guess.'

So the following day I sat down with Holly and Nevada at morning break-time and Holly pulled out her notepad and pen. 'OK,' she said in a heading-up-the-investigation sort of voice, 'so how are we going to do this?'

'It's elementary, my dear Watson,' I replied. (Holly and I have a bit of a Sherlock Holmes and Dr Watson thing going on at times like this, with the only trouble being that we *both* want to be Sherlock Holmes.) 'Clearly the *first* thing we need to do is check Matthew's alibi.'

She frowned. 'I thought you said he was with Jennifer.'

'I know – but we've only got *his* word for it. I reckon I'd better interview Jennifer as well.'

'I'll interview Matthew then,' Holly offered at once.

'I've already got a full statement from him,' I said quickly (not liking to imagine my brother's reaction if Holly suddenly descended on him with her notepad and pen). 'Anyway, I reckon the next person we need to interview is our chief suspect.'

'You mean *Ian*?' Holly sounded sceptical.

'Yes. I'll ask Jake where he lives, and then I think we should *all* go round to his house. I'll go and knock on his door and the two of you can wait outside in case I need back-up.'

Nevada was staring at me as if she thought I was mad. 'You really think he's going to talk to you?'

'Well, it's worth a shot. And the other thing we have to do is get a sample of his handwriting to compare it with the writing in that letter that was put through our door. Maybe you two should go through his rubbish bin while I'm distracting him with my interview.'

'Yeah – like *that's* really gonna happen,' Holly said, giving me a *get lost* sort of look. Nevada looked relieved, and as the school bell rang to signal the end of break-time Holly glanced at her and added, 'There *is* just one other thing I was wondering, Esmie. If the two of us are Sherlock Holmes and Doctor Watson, then who's Nevada going to be?' She had a gleam in her eye as she spoke, as if she already knew the answer.

It didn't take long for me to get what she was thinking. 'Moriarty!' I exclaimed.

She started to laugh. 'It's brilliant, isn't it?'

'But that's just my real surname,' Nevada said, sounding puzzled.

'Moriarty was *also* one of the characters in the Sherlock Holmes stories,' I explained to her quickly.

'Really?' She sounded pleased. 'I didn't know that. Was *he* a detective too then?'

'No,' Holly said, giggling. 'He was Sherlock Holmes's nemesis – his evil foe. Isn't that right, Esmie?'

I nodded. 'It's just kind of funny that you've got the same name as him.'

But Nevada didn't look as if she found it funny. In fact, from the way she was scowling, you'd think we had just told her that there was no place for her in our detective story at all.

At lunchtime I phoned Jennifer on her mobile and she confirmed that Matthew *had* been with her after school on Monday, which was the day the van had been painted. However, there was a short window of time that wasn't accounted for, so unfortunately Matty's alibi wasn't as air-tight as it had first seemed. When I told Jennifer my theory about Ian setting Matty up, she didn't seem to think it was a possibility. 'He's never liked Matthew, but I'm sure he'd never do anything like that.' She didn't have Ian's address – or maybe she just didn't want to give it to me – so as soon as I'd ended the call I set off to find Jake.

I found him in the school canteen with Matthew, and when I explained why I wanted Ian's address, Matty told him not to give it to me. 'I don't want you getting into any trouble on my account, Esmie. Dad's calmed down a lot since I managed to get the paint off the van. It's easier just to let him think it *was* me and be done with it.'

'But, Matty, that's not the point,' I protested. 'If you're innocent it's not right that you're taking the blame.'

'Look, there's plenty of stuff I've done in the past that Dad *hasn't* found out about,' he said, 'so I reckon it all evens out in the end. Just leave it, Esmie, OK?'

'I'm not leaving it,' I said doggedly. 'I'm going to go and see Ian and I'm going to *make* him tell the truth.'

'Well, you'll have to wait until he gets back then,' Jake put in. 'He's gone to see his dad in Manchester. He went on Monday morning.'

I stared at him. 'But he phoned Jennifer on Monday afternoon while Matthew was round there . . .'

'So? They do *have* phones in Manchester, you know,' Jake said sarcastically. 'And haven't you heard of mobiles?'

'You're sure he's been in Manchester for the last two days?' I asked.

'Of course I'm sure. Why?'

Matthew answered for me. 'Because if Ian went to Manchester on Monday morning he can't be the one who painted Robert's van on Monday night.' He turned to me and added, 'So thanks for trying to help, Ez, but it looks like you're on the wrong track.'

'As usual,' Jake quipped.

I went back to Holly and Nevada in a bit of a daze, not certain what to do next. My chief suspect had a rock-solid alibi and I didn't have a clue who else might have done it. In fact it looked horribly like I had come to a complete dead end.

'If this was a detective story like the ones you get on television, the culprit would be the person you *least* suspect,' Nevada said.

'Yes, but Esmie's dad always says that in real life it's often the person you suspect *most* who turns out to have done it,' Holly informed her. 'Only sometimes it's really hard to actually prove it. Isn't that right, Esmie?'

I nodded. The person I suspected most was still Ian and I was about to voice the possibility that Ian might have set up the crime but got someone else to do his dirty work for him – sort of like employing a hit-man if you didn't want to do your own murder. But before I could say anything Nevada suddenly asked Holly if she could come round to Holly's house with me that afternoon after school.

Holly looked shocked and she replied

straight away that she wasn't allowed to bring friends home without asking her mum first.

So Nevada got out her mobile and phoned up her aunt. 'Aunt Ruth, can you phone Holly's mum and ask if it's OK for me to go round there after school today?' she asked as Holly and I watched in amazement. She listened for a moment and said, 'Well, Holly's right here – I'll get her to tell you the number.' And then she was handing Holly the phone saying, 'Aunt Ruth wants to know your phone number.'

And after that it was a done deal, because there was no way Holly's mum was going to say no. (In fact she's always nagging Holly and me to get to know other people at school instead of just staying glued to each other the whole time.)

I didn't mind too much that Nevada had arranged for the three of us to hang out together after school for the second day in a row – but Holly was clearly furious about it.

'It's my own fault for being too friendly towards her,' Holly whispered when she got me to herself in French. 'Now she thinks we're going to include her in everything we do – well she's wrong.'

Holly pretty much ignored Nevada for the

whole of the walk back to her place, and she was still chatting almost exclusively to me as we sat in her bedroom at half past four, tucking in to the orange juice and biscuits her mum had brought upstairs for us. (Dad could learn a lot from Holly's mother, I reckon.)

Nevada listened to us in silence for a while, then she suddenly announced, 'By the way, I've got something to tell you.'

'What?' I asked through a mouthful of chocolate-chip cookie.

'It's about our case.' She paused dramatically. 'I think I know who did it.'

'Who?' Holly and I both asked at once.

'I can't say yet, not until I know for sure – but I'm almost positive I'm right.'

'Have you been getting psychic vibes about it?' I asked, starting to feel both excited and spooked at the same time.

But before Nevada could answer, Holly said dismissively, 'Of course she hasn't – she's just bluffing.'

'I am not!' Nevada retorted hotly. 'I just had a vision about it.'

'What sort of vision?' I asked.

But Holly was scornful. 'Don't be stupid, Esmie. She's making it up.'

'No I'm not,' Nevada protested.

'Oh yeah? Well, prove it then!'

'OK – I will. My psychic powers tell me that it's going to happen again very soon. So you'd better watch out!' She stood up and started to put on her coat. 'See you tomorrow, Esmie.'

'Nevada, don't leave –' I began, but she had clearly already made up her mind.

'She's definitely bluffing,' Holly said after she'd gone. 'Either that or she'll go and paint something herself to make it *look* like she was right.'

I was shocked. 'Do you really think she'd do that?'

'I think she'd do anything to get your attention.'

And I started to think about my mother's jewellery box and how Nevada had certainly grabbed my attention with *that*.

For the rest of the time I was at Holly's house she became more and more fixed on the idea that we couldn't trust Nevada. She even started to say that maybe Nevada was the one who had painted the fruit-and-veg van in the first place. 'Think about it, Esmie. She had the opportunity because she lives in your road and she knew all about Matthew painting her uncle's car, so that probably gave her the idea. And the van got painted the *same* evening she was in a huff with you because you came back to mine after school instead of going to hers.'

'But there's no way she'd do that, Holly!' I exclaimed. 'She's my friend.'

'That's just it – she *wants* to be your friend really badly, doesn't she? And as soon as you saw her after that van got painted, you were asking her if she could use her psychic powers to help solve the crime. Don't you see? Painting the van gave her a way of getting to hang out with you.'

I frowned. 'Yes, but what about that note? Why would she have written that?'

'I don't know. Maybe Ian really *did* write that and the two things aren't connected.'

'I don't think so, Holly,' I said, because this was all starting to sound way too complicated now.

'Well, I have a very strong hunch that I'm right,' Holly said firmly. 'And you're the one who's always saying that detectives ought to act more on their hunches.'

Dad collected me on his way home from work and I didn't have much time to think about what Holly had said, because as soon as we got through our front door, Matthew yelled downstairs to me that Grandma had just called from Chicago. 'She said she had something to tell you!'

'Can I phone her back straight away, Dad?'
I asked.

'All right. But I'm about to start dinner, so
don't be too long.'

I was going up the stairs so that I could use
the phone in Dad's room, when our doorbell
rang. I really hoped it was Lizzie – even though
I knew we weren't expecting her that night. I
paused on the stairs just to make sure it *wasn't*
her – and it turned out to be Steve, one of
Dad's policemen mates, who was still in his uniform and who had come to talk to Dad about
something to do with work.

'Hi, Steve,' I called down to him. Steve has
known Dad for a long time, and he and his wife
have got two boys the same ages as Matty and
me.

'Hi, Esmie. Still want to be a detective when
you grow up?' Steve asked me. (All Dad's
friends from work seem to know about that.)

'Of course,' I replied. 'I'm doing some
detective work at the moment actually – I'm
just going to call one of my informants.'

Dad invited him into the kitchen and asked
him if he wanted a cup of coffee, so I guessed
we were going to have to wait a while for our
dinner.

I didn't mind because it gave me more time
to phone Grandma. I couldn't think what it

was she had to tell me, but I guessed it must be connected with my mother's message.

I was right. As soon as Grandma picked up the phone, she started to tell me that ever since I had last called, she had been thinking a lot about my mum and those summer holidays in Brighton.

'I started to think about Amanda and Kirsten and I suddenly remembered that I might still have an address for their mother. She'd moved away from Brighton and we'd lost touch completely by the time Claire . . . well, by the time you were born. But I never throw out old address books, so I got them out and started to look through them. And I found her address – crossed out but still legible, so I've written to her and asked for Amanda and Kirsten's contact details. If she gets back to me I'll let you know.'

'Oh, I hope she does!' I gushed. 'Then we can ask Kirsten and Amanda all about the Mysterious Four Club – and what November the twenty-first means.'

'Yes, well don't get your hopes up too much. My letter might not ever reach them. That address must be at least fifteen years old by now!'

'I'm sure it'll get there,' I said. 'I've got a really good feeling about it.' And I really *did* have a good feeling – though since I'm not psychic I guess I probably shouldn't have counted on it as much as I did.

I was so excited when I came off the phone that I really wanted to tell someone – and since Nevada was the only other person who knew about my mother's message, I decided to pay her a visit. Plus I figured it would be good to have a talk with her sooner rather than later about what had happened at Holly's.

I went downstairs and called out to Dad that I was going over to Nevada's house for ten minutes. Dad was still talking with Steve in the kitchen, so I reckoned he wouldn't mind.

As I stepped outside I saw the police car Steve had parked in front of our house and I instantly froze.

Someone had painted in big red letters on the white bonnet *M H WAS HERE*.

My legs felt wobbly as I walked down our drive to the car and touched the paint. It was still wet, which meant it must have only just been done. It looked identical to the red paint that had been used on the fruit-and-veg van, and yet I knew Dad had locked that paint in a cupboard in our garage.

M H could only stand for one thing – *Matthew Harvey*. But there was no way my brother could have done this. OK, so he'd had the *opportunity* to slip out unnoticed while I was on the phone to Grandma, but that wasn't the point. The point was that there was no way in a million years that my brother would ever deface a police car.

I stood on the pavement, looking up and down the street to see if the person who had done this was still around. And that's when I saw a figure in the Stevens's driveway – Nevada was standing there watching me. As soon as she realized I'd spotted her, she turned and disappeared through the side gate that led round to the back of the house. And I instantly remembered what Holly had said earlier – that Nevada would probably paint something herself to make it *look* like she was psychic.

I ran over to her house and rattled the gate, but it must have been bolted from the garden side. 'Nevada!' I called out loudly.

There was no reply, but I was too wound up to leave it there, and without stopping to think what might happen next, I marched up the steps on to the porch and rang the front doorbell.

❦ 19 ❦

The mistake I made, I realized afterwards, was blaming Nevada the second she came to the door, instead of questioning her some more first. But as I stood on the porch waiting to be let in I could hear raised voices inside the house, and when Nevada opened the door to me, I saw straight away that she had a smear of red paint on one hand.

'Holly was right – it *is* you!' I burst out, staring at the paint. And instead of skilfully interviewing her to get the confession I wanted, I just yelled at her until she slammed the door in my face.

'I bet you made up all that other stuff just to get my attention as well,' I shouted through the letter box. 'I don't know how you did it – but I bet you're a total fake and I bet your mum is too!'

She opened the door again so suddenly that I nearly fell into the house. 'My mum is *not* a fake and neither am I,' she hissed. 'And you still need me to tell you what that message means, so you'd better shut up!'

'I don't need you to tell me anything,' I retorted. 'My grandma's written to Kirsten and Amanda and they're going to tell me all about it.'

'By the time *they* get back to you it'll be too late!' she snapped, slamming the door shut all over again.

I was trembling when I got back to our house, and as I entered the hall, Dad and Steve were emerging from the kitchen.

Dad took one look at me and asked, 'Esmie, what's wrong?'

'Steve's car . . .' I mumbled, pointing outside. 'But it wasn't Matty. It was Nevada.'

'What are you talking about?'

I led them out on to the drive so they could see for themselves, and Steve swore under his breath when he saw the state of his car.

Dad looked shocked. For a moment I thought he was too angry to speak, but then he seemed to pull himself together. 'It's OK, Steve. The paint's probably just emulsion – it should come off with water.'

Steve had already gone to take a closer look.

'You know who did this then?' he asked in surprise.

'Let's just say it's happened before,' Dad replied. He sounded scarily calm as he said, 'Esmie, go and get your brother.'

'But Matty didn't do it, Dad. I told you. It was Nevada. She even had paint on her hand.' And for some reason my tea-leaf reading came flashing into my mind – *A friend in whom you trusted will prove false*.

'Just get him please,' Dad said firmly.

But Matthew was already on his way downstairs. 'What's going on?' he asked me as we met in the hall.

'It's happened again, Matty,' I said. 'Nevada did it, but she won't confess.'

Matthew followed me outside and gazed at the police car in disbelief. Dad and Steve were both watching him closely.

'Dad, you can't think *I* did this!' he burst out.

'You're *M H* aren't you?' Dad said sternly.

'Yes, but I didn't write that!'

Dad didn't say anything. He was looking at my brother's face very carefully, as if he was trying to decide whether Matty was lying or not.

'Dad, it wasn't me!' Matthew exclaimed again. 'Look, if it was, do you really think I'd be stupid enough to put my own initials?'

'You might if you were trying to send me a message,' Dad said.

'What message?' Matthew looked perplexed. 'What are you talking about? Look, I'm telling you, Dad, I would never do this. I mean it's a *police* car.'

'And it's *my* police car,' Steve grunted. 'So you'd better *not* have done it or you'll be getting a right good kick in the backside from *me* as well as your dad.'

'Steve, I *didn't* do it, honestly.'

Dad was looking at my brother with an expression I couldn't quite fathom. Then he said slowly, 'I think I believe you.'

'Dad I'm telling you—' Matty began, breaking off abruptly as he took in what Dad had just said. 'You *do*?'

'Yes. I actually don't think you *would* do this.' He paused. 'Please tell me I'm not wrong.'

Matthew shook his head emphatically. 'No, Dad, you're not. Of course you're not.' And I could tell that he couldn't quite believe that Dad was on his side at last.

'Well, thank God for that,' Steve said gruffly.

'Matty didn't paint that van either, Dad,' I added. 'That must have been Nevada too, just like Holly said.'

'Well, regardless of what Holly says, I think we'd better not jump to any conclusions.' Dad turned to speak to Steve. 'Look, I'm really sorry about this, but I'll get to the bottom of it and let you know what I find out.'

Steve nodded. 'Here's you thinking you'd finished work for the day, eh?'

Dad grimaced. 'Come on. We'd better get this paint cleaned off before you go back to the station.'

'At least Lizzie doesn't have to worry that Matty's been vandalizing stuff because he doesn't want her moving in with us,' I said after we'd waved Steve on his way.

We were all in the kitchen, and Dad was checking to see what food we had in the fridge. 'How do you know about that?' he asked.

'Well . . .'

'I didn't know Lizzie thought that,' Matthew said. He had been munching his way through a jumbo bag of crisps, having clearly regained his appetite.

Dad seemed to forget that he had just asked me a question and instead he turned to look at my brother. 'Actually I was beginning to think that too, Matthew. I mean . . . how *do* you feel about Lizzie moving in?'

Matthew shrugged. 'I think it's cool.'

'You said before that you thought she was unreliable,' I reminded him.

'No I didn't.'

'Yes you did. You said *all* women are unreliable.'

Dad frowned. 'Matthew, I really don't think that at sixteen you can call yourself an expert on all women!'

'I never said I was.'

'Well, you shouldn't have said they were all unreliable then,' I told him.

'Look, I was just talking about Jennifer. And . . . and . . .' He swallowed and looked nervously at Dad. 'I just meant Jennifer, OK.'

'Yes, well I hope you didn't mean our mum as well,' I said, giving him a stern look. 'Because I don't think you can call dying in childbirth *unreliable*, can you, Dad?'

Dad looked taken aback, then to my surprise he started to smile. 'I agree, Esmie. You can call it many things, but *unreliable* probably isn't one of them.'

'Of course I didn't mean her,' Matthew told me huffily.

'Then why did you put away her photo?' I demanded.

'I don't know. I just felt . . .' He swallowed and didn't seem to be able to go on.

'Angry?' Dad suggested gently.

Matthew looked at him in surprise. 'I guess I just felt mad because of Jennifer dumping me. I'm not angry about Lizzie moving in if that's what you're thinking. I *want* the two of you to be together. I told you before. It's cool.'

'Well, thank you. That's good to know,' Dad said softly. 'And, Matthew – *wherever* you decide to keep your mother's picture is fine with me. I know you don't need a photograph in order to remember her.'

I felt a bit uncomfortable when Dad said that, because unlike Matthew I *do* need a photograph or I wouldn't have any picture of my mother inside my head at all.

'Can I phone Lizzie and tell her what's happened, Dad?' I asked. 'Then maybe she'll come home . . . I mean *back*,' I added quickly. After all this wasn't, strictly speaking, Lizzie's home yet – not while she still had her own flat.

'I think I'll do that myself, thanks, Esmie,' Dad replied. 'In fact how about I phone her now, while you two make a start on tea?'

However, he didn't have time to phone, because at that moment our doorbell rang. Matty and I stayed in the kitchen while Dad went to answer it, and straight away we heard Mr Stevens's voice. 'Sorry to disturb you, but my niece has something she wants to tell you.'

We both rushed into the hall, expecting to see Nevada, but as Dad invited Mr Stevens inside, we saw that the only person with him, looking incredibly sulky, was Carys.

As soon as we were all seated in the living room, we turned towards her expectantly, but the only one *she* was looking at was my brother.

'It wasn't Nevada who painted that police car and the van,' she told him frostily. 'It was me. And it was me who sent that letter to your dad, in case you haven't worked that out by now.'

I gasped. Not only had I been wrong about Nevada, I'd been wrong about Ian putting that note through the door. 'But how did you know all the stuff you put in that letter?' I asked her, feeling confused.

She looked at me scornfully. '*You* told Nevada about the school sign – and *she* told me. And I actually *saw* Matthew and his mate painting Uncle's Frank car. I mean, how dumb is that? At least when *I* did it I made sure nobody was about! *And* I used paint that would wash off.'

'But . . . but *why*?' Matthew blurted.

'Why do you think?' she hissed.

And of course it was obvious then – at least it was to me.

'Because I don't like being used and tossed away like some piece of garbage,' Carys told him angrily. 'You asked me out on that date just so that you could make your old girlfriend jealous. Nevada told me all about your little plan afterwards.' She glowered at me then. 'I hear *you* had quite a lot to do with it too.'

I blushed. Nevada had said that Carys would get over my brother dropping her – but clearly she was wrong. 'It was Nevada's idea, not mine!' I protested, but Dad gave me a sharp look and I quickly stared at my shoes.

'Matthew,' Dad said sternly. 'Explain, please.'

'Well . . . it . . . it's true that I did want to make Jennifer jealous . . .' He was flushing guiltily. 'But I didn't think Carys would mind so much.'

'You didn't think I'd *mind*?' Carys snarled. 'What are you? Some kind of moron?'

'That's still no excuse for doing what you did, Carys,' Mr Stevens put in quickly. He turned to Dad. 'The two of them are as bad as each other, wouldn't you say?'

Dad ignored him and asked Carys a few more questions. Apparently she'd taken the red paint from Mr Stevens's garden shed, and I was right about her having planted the paint pot and brush in our garage to incriminate Matthew.

'I haven't heard you apologize yet, Carys,'

Mr Stevens told her. 'That's what we came here for, in case you've forgotten.'

'Yeah, well I haven't heard *him* apologize yet either,' Carys retorted, glaring at my brother.

Matthew looked angry. 'I don't see why I should – *you've* done worse than me.'

'Well *you* started it! You know I really enjoyed it when your dad brought you over to our place and made *you* apologize. You looked *so* ashamed of yourself – quite right too. It's a good job your dad's so strict with you, because you obviously need it.'

'*You* can talk!' Matthew exclaimed indignantly.

'OK – that's enough, both of you!' Dad said sharply, and Mr Stevens clearly thought so too, because he hastily suggested that it was time he and Carys left.

As Dad showed them out, Carys was the last to leave the room, and on her way to the door she paused to pull an envelope out of her pocket. 'Here,' she said, tossing it to me. 'It's from Nevada. She had paint on her hands when you saw her because she was trying to grab the paint pot off me. She's pretty mad at you for thinking she did it.'

'Tell her I'm sorry,' I mumbled.

'Tell her yourself. She *might* even still want

to be friends with you. She's pretty weird that way.'

Luckily Matthew was fuming too much to bother to ask what was in the envelope, and I had stuffed it unopened into my pocket by the time Dad came back into the room.

'It's not fair, Dad,' Matthew burst out immediately. '*She's* the one who did something wrong and I'm the one everyone's having a go at.'

Dad looked exasperated. 'What she did *was* wrong, Matthew – but quite frankly I can see why she wanted to get her own back. I mean, do you really think that's the right way to treat girls?'

'See what I mean? Now *I'm* the one in trouble! It's not fair!'

'Look, calm down and just listen, will you?' Dad said firmly, and I could tell he was getting all geared up for a major father-and-son talk.

I decided now would be a good time to leave them to it. Besides, I still had to open Nevada's letter.

I felt incredibly nervous as I sat on my bed and undid the envelope. There was a sheet of paper inside, with something written on it in Nevada's neat handwriting. It said: *Your mum wants to meet you at the end of the pier in Brighton on 21st November – that's what the message means. But you can't tell anyone or she won't be there.*

I stared at the note, starting to feel my spine tingle. The twenty-first of November was this Saturday – three days away. But my mother couldn't really be there to meet me – that was just crazy. I mean, OK, so Nevada was clearly talking about her *spirit* form – but that was still impossible.

Or was it? I looked at my mother's photograph and I could almost swear that her eyes were smiling at me just a tiny bit more than usual. Of course, I was probably just imagining it, but still . . .

• 20 •

I was convinced that everything was going to be fine as soon as Dad phoned Lizzie – but it turned out that it wasn't.

When he eventually managed to call her, Lizzie wasn't at home, so he tried her mobile. She answered that, and he found out that she had gone to stay with a friend for a few days.

'But what about her job?' I asked when Dad told us.

'I think she's taken some leave.'

'Pulled a sicky you mean,' Matthew quipped.

'I don't know about that, but she won't be back until the weekend. Then she says she's got something to tell us.'

'*What?*' I asked, getting a sudden tight feeling in my chest.

'I hope she's not going to dump you, Dad,' Matty said, sounding worried, 'though I guess if she was, she wouldn't say she had something to tell all of us, would she?'

'She might,' I said, frowning. Lizzie is a lot more sensitive than Dad, so she'd probably realize that by dumping *him* she'd really be dumping Matty and me as well.

'Yes, well, let's try not to speculate too much at this stage, shall we, guys?' Dad said drily.

But I couldn't stop thinking about it, and the more I thought, the more worried I became. On Friday when I got home from school (our school doesn't do detention on Fridays, so Matty was home too), I went to the cupboard and my gaze fell on a fresh packet of loose-leaf China tea. Lizzie's the only one in our house who drinks anything other than tea bags, so I guessed it must be hers.

That was what gave me the idea, and before I had time to change my mind, I was opening the packet of tea and getting out a suitable cup. My tea-leaf reading had proved true before, hadn't it? So maybe if I did it again it would tell me what was happening with Lizzie.

I put a spoonful of the loose leaves into my cup and, when the kettle had boiled, I poured the water on. I drank it slowly, until only about a teaspoonful of liquid was left, then I held it in my left hand and moved it in a circle three times in an anticlockwise direction. And while I was doing that I concentrated as hard as I could on my question.

When I reckoned I had waited long enough, I turned the cup over on to the saucer and left it there for a few minutes to let the liquid drain away. Finally I took hold of the cup's handle with my right hand, turned it upright again and peered down at the pattern the tea leaves had made.

I stared at them for a long time. There were two main areas on the cup where the leaves had settled, but I couldn't make out a picture in either one of them.

If only Nevada was here, I thought.

I found myself going over to our front window, still holding the teacup. I could see lights on in the Stevens's house. Mr Stevens's car wasn't in the drive, so I figured now might be a good time to go over there and apologize to Nevada. Of course, she might not want to speak to me, but it was worth a try. After all, she *had* sent me that message via her sister, so it was possible that she wasn't as angry with me as I thought, even though we had been avoiding each other at school.

I sneaked out of the house without telling Matthew where I was going, and rang the Stevens's front doorbell, clutching the teacup in my right hand. (I had been careful not to transfer it to my left one in case that ruined the reading.)

Carys answered the door. 'Oh, it's you.'

'I need to speak to Nevada, please. Is she in?'

'Yeah, but I'm not sure she'll want to speak to you. NEVADA!' she yelled up the stairs. Then she disappeared into the living room and slammed the door.

Nevada came to the top of the stairs and peered down at me.

'Nevada, I've come to say I'm sorry I accused you of painting that police car,' I said at once. 'And I *don't* think you and your mum are frauds. And . . . and I wondered if you could help me read these tea leaves.' I held up the cup so she could see it.

'You're doing another reading?' She sounded surprised.

'Yes, but I can't make anything out.'

She was descending the stairs now, with a smug expression on her face. 'I thought you didn't believe in psychic stuff any more.'

'I just got a bit freaked out by everything, I guess. But there's something going on with Lizzie and I really want to know what it is.'

She reached the bottom of the stairs and told me to twist the cup round for her to have a look inside. 'There are two connected pictures,' she told me after she'd stared at the tea leaves for a minute or two. 'There's a horse's head there, see – and that black clump behind it is a carriage. And over here you can see lots of shapes that represent people. And there's a long rectangle – that always means a coffin.'

'A coffin?' I was horrified.

'Yes – one picture is a hearse and the other is a funeral.'

'That can't be right!' But as I stared into the cup, I started to see what she meant.

At that moment the front door opened and Nevada's aunt walked into the hall – and before she had time to ask me what I was doing there, I rushed past her and out of the house.

As soon as I got home I held the cup under the kitchen tap until all the tea leaves had rinsed away. But I still felt terrible. Lizzie couldn't be going to die! And suddenly I had a truly awful thought. What if that was the thing that Lizzie was about to tell us? I mean, what if she had just found out that she had a terminal illness or something?

I quickly told myself that couldn't be true. If Lizzie was ill then she'd be losing weight or going to lots of hospital appointments or something. The hearse and the funeral must mean something else.

Just then the phone rang and I picked it up straight away, guessing it might be Nevada.

I was right. 'You've *got* to go to Brighton on

November the twenty-first, Esmie. That's what that reading means. It's your mother's spirit letting you know that if you don't go, something terrible will happen.'

'But November the twenty-first is tomorrow,' I said.

'You *have* to go.' She lowered her voice. 'I'll come with you if you like – I can tell my aunt and uncle I'm going over to your place for the day.'

My hand was shaking when I finally put down the phone. I knew how to get to Brighton because Dad had taken Matthew and me there lots of times before, but still . . . only a mad person would agree to what Nevada had just suggested.

The next day was a Saturday, and luckily Dad was working, which meant that Matthew was looking after me.

'I don't mind if you want to see Jennifer today,' I told my brother as soon as Dad had left. 'I'll stay in and watch TV and I won't tell Dad you went out, I promise.'

'Yeah, but it's a bit risky. Maybe I should just get Jennifer to come round here for a bit.'

'Why don't you go round to hers? Her dad works on a Saturday, doesn't he? Then I can ask Holly to come over, and we won't all be fighting about what to watch on TV.'

'Well . . .'

'Go on, Matty. The two of you are always hanging out here. You don't want her to get bored with you again, do you?'

That seemed to do the trick. 'Well, I suppose you'd know where I was if anything happened. And I guess Dad wouldn't find out if I took her tenpin bowling before she goes to work this afternoon, would he? She's been going on about wanting to do that.'

'Why don't you go round there now? You can spend the whole day with her if you like. I don't mind.'

I waited until he had left, then I wrote him a note telling him I'd be back by the time Dad got home, because I guessed he might return to the house before I did and panic when he found me missing. Then I put on my warmest coat, scarf, hat and gloves, and headed for Nevada's house. She must have been looking out for me, because she opened the front door as soon as I got there.

'I've told Aunt Ruth we're going to the park and then going back to your place,' she said. 'Have you got your mobile with you?'

I nodded. 'But I'm switching it off in case Matty tries to ring.'

'Carys has been asking a lot of questions. I think she knows something's up, so we'd better hurry.'

'Come on,' I said. 'I know a short cut to the station.'

Dad had taken Matty and me to Brighton by train on a number of occasions because it was so convenient. You can travel from our local station to London Victoria in just under an hour, and then get another train directly to Brighton. You can also buy a ticket for the whole journey at our local ticket office, which means that when you arrive in London, all you have to do is look at the Departures board and find out which platform the Brighton train is leaving from.

Our plan was to spend a couple of hours in Brighton – during which time we would visit the pier. Then we would catch the train back, and with any luck be home by the time Dad got in at six. Nevada had told her aunt that she was staying at mine all day, so hopefully nobody would come looking for her.

The first thing that went wrong happened before we'd even set off. We had bought our tickets (I had spent all the money I'd been saving up for Christmas) and I had left Nevada on the platform while I went to use the Ladies' Room.

But when I came back afterwards, Carys was there.

'She followed us from the house,' Nevada explained crossly when I joined them. 'I've told her we're only going a couple of stops on the train and that we're visiting one of your friends, but she's kicking up a big fuss about it.'

'You told Aunt Ruth you were going to the park. You can't just take off somewhere completely different.' Carys was glaring at her sister. 'She's already upset enough with me as it is, and if *you* do *this*, she might change her mind about letting us stay. And there's no way I'm going to live in Saudi Arabia.'

'Esmie, maybe we should leave it for today,' Nevada said apologetically.

'But I can't,' I said, surprised by how strongly I felt about it. 'Anyway we've already got the tickets. Look, I'll go on my own and I'll let you know what happens.'

Nevada looked shocked – as if she hadn't expected me to want to go to Brighton without her – but I knew that for me there was no going back.

I must have been in a sort of daze for most of the journey, because I can hardly remember any of it now. But I do remember how I felt when I finally walked out of the station in Brighton. I felt very scared and very cold.

It was really windy, especially when I got to the seafront, and it was a much longer walk to the pier than I remembered. Last time I'd been there it had been summer, and Dad had bought us ice creams, which we'd eaten sitting on deckchairs looking out to sea. Today I had my duffel coat buttoned up to my neck and woolly tights on under my jeans, and I was *still* freezing.

When I finally got to the pier, I stood at the entrance, thinking how different it must have looked when my mother was a girl. There were a few people outside on the pier walkway, though I guessed most were inside enjoying all the amusements. Slowly I started to walk along the promenade towards the far end of the pier, and as I passed the section where most of the rides were I remembered the last time I'd been there when I'd had a go on the big helter-skelter and the dodgems. I passed a shop selling ice creams and went in and bought a Mr Whippy with strawberry sauce. It was windy and the ice cream soon started to drip all over me.

There was no one at the very end of the pier when I got there, although there was a seagull perched on the railing, and for a creepy moment I let myself imagine that the seagull was my mum – or at least her spirit come back to visit me in bird form. But several more sea-gulls soon appeared, all of them shrieking and flapping their wings, and I soon went off that idea.

I had brought the message my mother had written and now I took it out of my pocket, clutching it tightly to make sure it didn't blow away. It seemed to me that I had done every-thing correctly. It was the twenty-first of November (the special date), I was on the pier (the special place) and I was holding a whirly ice cream (the secret sign). Plus my own name *was* the secret password.

I stood there, facing out to sea, with the wind whipping round me, letting the ice cream run down on to my hand. I closed my eyes and tried to imagine my mother as she looks in the photographs we have of her at home. Maybe if I concentrated really hard on visualizing her face, something would happen.

But the only thing that happened was that I started to feel an incredibly achy longing-for-someone-who-isn't-there sort of feeling, almost as if my mother had only just died.

I waited at the end of the pier for a whole hour, and by that time I had given up hope that anything out of the ordinary was going to occur. In fact I was starting to feel really stupid, and home felt like a very long way away. I looked at my watch and realized I would have to leave soon if I wanted to have any chance of being back before Dad.

And that's when something really weird happened.

A dog came running towards me, barking. It was a brown spaniel and someone was calling after it, 'RUSTY! Come here!' Then a lady in a bright red headscarf appeared, and the dog turned and ran back to her, and they both walked away along the pier together.

I stared after them. Rusty was the name of the dog in the Mysterious Four Club.

It was then that I heard someone calling my name. At first I thought I was just imagining it, but then I heard it again. It was a female voice – difficult to hear clearly above the wind, but it was definitely real.

❧ 21 ❧

'Esmie, thank goodness! Are you all right?'

It was Lizzie.

I stared at her. I couldn't speak.

'Nevada said you'd be here. We've been trying to phone you all day. Matthew went back to the house and got worried when he found your note. Esmie, you can't just go tearing off to Brighton on your own! What were you thinking?' She was taking her phone out of her pocket now.

'Are you phoning Matthew?'

'I'm calling your father. He's very worried about you, but since he's very busy at work he actually agreed to let *me* come and find you.'

'Really?' I was surprised. One of the things that Dad and Lizzie sometimes argue about is the way that Dad can't seem to totally trust anyone else – not even Lizzie – when it comes to anything important to do with Matty and me. This was the first time he'd delegated such a major task to her.

'Matthew was too scared to phone your dad at first, so he phoned me instead. We contacted Holly and Nevada, thinking you might be with them, and Nevada told us you'd come here.' She started speaking into the phone now. 'I've found her, John. Don't worry – she's fine. She's on the pier. I'll bring her straight home.'

I was dreading that Dad was going to want to speak to me, but he didn't. Lizzie came off the phone and frowned. 'You look freezing. And you've spilt ice cream all down your coat. How on earth can you eat ice cream on a day like this? Come on. Let's go and find the car. I was in such a state when I parked it, I just hope I can remember where it is.'

'There was a dog,' I mumbled, looking around for it as we walked back along the pier together. 'Did you see it? It was called Rusty. I thought it was a sign.'

Lizzie looked puzzled. 'What do you mean?'

I shook my head, not wanting to answer. The whole thing seemed stupid now. And I suddenly felt so glad that she had come to find me that I burst into tears.

'Oh, Esmie,' Lizzie murmured, putting her arm round me and hugging me tightly, and I realized that *she* was on the verge of tears too.

*

Needless to say, Dad was really angry with me when I got home, and I had to tell him everything. Apparently all Nevada had said was that I'd told her I was taking the train to Brighton because I wanted to go on the pier.

'But it was Nevada's idea,' I said, explaining how she was psychic and how she had told me that my mother's spirit wanted to meet me there.

'She told you *what*?' Dad sounded outraged.

'Look.' I showed him my mother's message and told him how Nevada had used her psychic powers to find the secret compartment in the jewellery box.

'Esmie, I can't believe you were taken in by all this hocus-pocus!' Dad exclaimed.

'It's *not* hocus-pocus!' I protested. 'Nevada was right about all the names of the Mysterious Four! And she sensed the secret compartment was there.'

'Yes, well I think we should go and speak to her about this right now,' Dad said grimly.

So I had no choice but to go with him to Nevada's house.

Carys answered the door.

'We'd like to speak to Nevada, please,' Dad said, 'and I think I'd better have a word with your aunt and uncle as well.'

'They're all out,' Carys replied. 'I see you

got back OK then, Esmie. I should have realized the two of you were lying when I saw you at the station.'

'The *two* of you?' Dad queried, looking at me.

'Nevada was supposed to come too,' I mumbled.

'Carys, could we come inside and talk about this?' Dad asked.

'Sure.' Carys turned and led us into the house. 'I only found out you were going to Brighton after Lizzie came over here looking for you, Esmie,' she said to me as she showed us into the living room. 'Nevada told us you were going to the pier, but she said she didn't know *why*. I knew she was holding something back, so after Lizzie left I made her tell me the whole story.'

'I'd be very grateful if you could tell the whole story to *me*, Carys,' Dad said. 'Why on earth would Nevada tell Esmie that her mother's spirit was going to meet her at the end of the pier?'

Carys sighed. 'She was just really desperate to get Esmie to spend some time with her away from Holly. She'd have invented some reason why your mum wasn't there when you got to the pier, Esmie, and then the two of you would have ended up spending the afternoon together.'

I gaped at her. 'You mean Nevada made it up about my mum?'

Carys nodded. 'But don't think too badly of her. This is the first time she's ever made such a good friend so quickly after we've moved anywhere. She's a bit obsessed with you, I think. And she's *really* jealous of how close you are to Holly.'

'Esmie seems to have got it into her head that your sister is psychic,' Dad said.

'Dad, she *is*,' I protested.

'How can you say that after what you've just heard?' He looked exasperated.

'But, Dad, she must be! How else would she have known all those names and been able to find the secret compartment in my jewellery box?'

Dad looked at Carys for help.

'There's something I think you need to see, Esmie,' she said. 'Wait here a minute.' She left the room and we heard her going upstairs.

When she returned she was carrying a big wooden jewellery box that was almost identical to my mother's.

'But . . . but . . .' I stared at it.

'Your mum's wasn't the only one of that kind that was made, you know. Our mum had this one when *she* was a kid. She gave it to me years ago and Nevada knows all about the false bottom. I guess when she saw yours and she realized you didn't know about it, she saw her chance to impress you.'

I was stunned as Carys demonstrated how if you pressed in the right place on the base of the box, the secret compartment was revealed. 'But . . . but how could she have known all those names?' I burst out. 'She told me those *before* we found the message inside.'

Carys looked thoughtful. 'Did you leave her alone with the box before you opened up the compartment together?'

'I don't think so . . . oh!' I suddenly remembered the day I had first shown Nevada the box. It was the same day she had seen the dwarf in my tea leaves.

She had instructed me to take my teacup out of the room, thus leaving *her* alone with the jewellery box. She could easily have opened the secret compartment, read the message (including the names), and put it back to be rediscovered later.

I shook my head, feeling terrible. 'Nevada wouldn't do that to me.'

'A lot of people who claim to be psychics are playing on the neediness of those who've lost loved ones, Esmie,' Dad said gently. 'You're not the first person to be fooled.'

'But what about when she showed me that crystal ball?' I asked shakily. 'She said she saw a wedding in it.'

'I'm sorry, Esmie,' Carys said. 'She must

have been making it up. Only our mother can see things in that crystal ball.'

'Well . . . well, what about my tea-leaf reading?' I blurted. 'There really *was* a hearse and a funeral inside my cup because *I* saw them too.'

'Oh, well you don't have to be psychic to read tea leaves,' Carys said, sounding relieved that there was at least one thing her sister had done that she could vouch for. 'And you don't have to worry, Esmie, because both of those are good omens. A funeral means that great happiness lies ahead, and a hearse really does mean that there's going to be a wedding soon.'

'But that's really weird,' I pointed out.

Carys shrugged. 'The tea leaves just have a good sense of humour, I guess.'

'Or a good sense of how to mislead people,' Dad put in drily. 'Carys, do you have any idea when the others will be back tonight?'

'They went to the theatre. It finishes around ten, I think.'

'Well, will you tell them I'll call round tomorrow to have a talk with them?'

'Sure.' As she came with us to the front door she added, 'You know, my mum's a *true* psychic and she would never trick anyone. She really *does* have the gift.'

'Really?' Dad sounded like he didn't believe her.

I felt in a total daze as we crossed the road to go home, but there was still one hope I was clinging to. 'I know you don't believe in psychic things, Dad, but I really *did* see a hearse and a funeral inside my teacup.'

'The power of suggestion is a great thing, Esmie. I expect you'd have seen the entire London Philharmonic Orchestra if Nevada had told you it was there,' Dad replied briskly.

I frowned. 'Well, there was definitely a dog called Rusty at the end of the pier today. And you can't see a whole dog by the power of suggestion, can you?'

'No, but there's also the power of coincidence. I mean Rusty isn't exactly the most unusual name for a dog, is it?'

I would have continued arguing, but I suddenly remembered something else. 'Dad, what was it Lizzie wanted to talk to us about? I asked her in the car but she said she wanted *you* to tell me.'

'Oh, yes. Apparently the couple who agreed to rent her flat still want to buy it, and they've upped their offer. So she's thinking of selling, but that means she'd have to find a home for all her furniture. So she wants to know if we're up for changing the house round a bit to accommodate some of it. She wants to have some of her own things around her if she's going to move in properly and she was worried about how you and Matty might react to that. After all, you've both been acting rather oddly lately.'

'*I* haven't been acting oddly,' I protested. 'I *want* Lizzie to move in with us.'

'Yes, well, I think in your case she's more worried that if she tells you she's selling her flat you'll think that means she's going to marry me tomorrow.' He paused. 'It's not that we definitely won't *ever* be getting married, Esmie – it's just that we want to do things gradually. I'd like you to understand that and be a bit more patient, OK?'

I frowned, because I'm not very good at being patient. 'Does *Matty* know that she wants to sell her flat?'

'I told him while you and Lizzie were on your way back from Brighton.'

'What did he say?'

'Well, he was a bit concerned that Lizzie might want to replace our leather sofa with her flowery one, but basically he said it was cool.'

I nodded. 'It *is* cool.' And even though Dad had asked me to be patient, I couldn't help grinning to myself as I saw the bridesmaid's dress I wanted getting just a little bit closer.

22

The next day Dad said he wanted to go and speak to Nevada's aunt and uncle alone. He was over there for ages, and when he eventually came back, Nevada was with him.

'Nevada has some things she wants to say to you, Esmie,' Dad said, and he left us in the living room with the door open (so I knew for a fact he was listening in).

Nevada looked like she had been crying. 'I'm sorry I lied to you,' she said. 'I just wanted you to be my friend – that's all.'

I listened while she told me how she had done it – and the stuff with the jewellery box was just as I'd thought. The whole thing had been a trick.

'What about the tea leaves?' I asked hoarsely.

'Mum's taught me a lot of the symbols and what they mean. I . . . I looked for those things

– but you did see them too, Esmie, so it's not like they weren't there.'

'*A friend in whom you trusted will prove false,*' I said. 'You meant me to think that was Holly, didn't you?'

'I'm sorry.'

'Don't be – that reading was completely right. It was talking about *you*.'

'I only did it because I wanted to be your friend so badly,' she murmured.

'I'd have been your friend anyway,' I protested. 'I won't now though, and neither will Holly when I tell her what you did!'

She sniffed. 'It doesn't matter. I'm leaving next week.'

'Leaving?'

'I'm going to Saudi Arabia to be with Mum and Dad.'

'What . . . for good, you mean?'

She gave a bitter smile. 'It's never for good. That's why Carys is staying here with Aunt Ruth and Uncle Frank. She's desperate to settle down somewhere. So am I, but I just miss Mum and Dad too much.' Her voice was trembly as she said, 'Esmie, I know you miss your mum too. I'm so sorry I made you think I could put you in touch with her.'

I felt my eyes fill with tears and I quickly blinked them back. 'Don't worry,' I said harshly. 'I never *really* believed you anyway. My mother's dead – and dead people can't come back.'

'Esmie, I really wish I *did* have psychic powers,' she blurted. 'If I did, I promise I'd use them to help you.' She started to cry then. 'I know what I did was wrong but I just wanted you to need me as much as I needed you.'

And that's when Dad came back into the room and suggested it was time Nevada left.

I went with her to the door, and she was still crying as she stepped outside.

'I guess I'll see you in school,' I mumbled, starting to feel a tiny bit sorry for her.

She shook her head. 'Aunt Ruth says I don't have to go back. I'll be too busy getting ready to leave.'

I watched her walk down our drive and, as she stepped on to the pavement, I called out, 'There was a dog called Rusty at the end of the pier.'

She turned round. 'Really?'

'Yes.'

I watched her face brighten up just a little bit – and that was the last time I saw her.

After that, things in our house got back to normal – well, sort of.

I phoned Holly and told her the whole story,

and when I confided in her that I actually felt a little bit sorry for Nevada, she snorted dismissively. 'Esmie, she used your *dead mother* to manipulate you into being friends with her. You should have told her that that's the way to make enemies, not friends. If you ask me, she turned out to be a true Moriarty after all.'

So after that I didn't mention Nevada to Holly again.

We did talk about Nevada at home though – mostly instigated by Lizzie, who thinks it's healthier to talk about stressful things rather than just pretend they never happened (which is more Dad's way of thinking).

Of course, Dad had given both Matty and me a really stern talking-to about the whole Brighton incident – me for going off like that and Matty for leaving me in the house on my own.

'It wasn't Matty's fault, Dad,' I'd protested when he'd finished spelling out all the terrible things that might have happened to me.

'Matty disobeyed me,' Dad said firmly. 'And so did you. I'm very disappointed in you both.'

'I'm really sorry, Dad,' my brother said, hanging his head.

'So you should be. You're old enough to know better.'

Dad seemed to forgive us both fairly quickly

though, and the fact that Matty seemed to be trying for some sort of perfect-son award after that certainly helped. My brother seemed loads happier in general and he was acting very differently towards Dad. He was less cheeky, he listened more to what Dad told him and he hadn't been late home once since he'd stopped being grounded. His relationship with Jennifer was still a bit rocky, so there were days when he was in a bad mood about that – but instead of shutting himself in his room sulking, he had started hanging out downstairs with us and actually allowing us to try and cheer him up.

I asked Lizzie what she thought had caused the change in him, and she said she reckoned it had something to do with Dad believing him about that police car. 'I think it did Matty a lot of good to see that your dad had faith in him after all.'

As for me – Dad seemed more concerned about my emotional state after my trip to Brighton than the fact that I'd disobeyed him, and he even offered to take me to the doctor's to see the practice counsellor if I wanted.

'I'd rather just talk it over with you and Lizzie,' I told him. And I found myself asking if he was absolutely sure that there's no way a dead person can live on in spirit form.

'Well, I'm not at all religious, Esmie, you know that, so *I* believe that the dead can only live on in our memories.'

'But I don't *have* any memories of my mum,' I said, frowning.

'Well, perhaps what I mean is that they live on in our thoughts,' he said.

'Oh,' I said, liking the sound of that much better.

'Of course, a lot of people believe in heaven too,' Dad added.

I nodded. 'I've always believed my mum's in heaven.'

'I know – and that's fine. I just *don't* think it's fine to think that the spirits of the dead are all around us and can actually send us messages.'

'But what about Nevada's mum? She's a *real* psychic, isn't she?'

'Esmie, you know what I think about Nevada's mum.'

I did know, and I couldn't help feeling sad – like I'd had something really important in my grasp and lost it.

Dad came over and gave me a hug. 'You know, if you want to think about your mother, you should think about the real her and not some ghostlike fantasy.'

'But I didn't *know* the real her,' I pointed out impatiently.

'I realize that – so when your grandma comes over at Christmas we'll make a point of telling you everything we can remember about her and seeing if we can't bring her to life for you a bit better. How's that?'

I really liked the sound of that, but at the same time I was worried about something. 'Won't Lizzie mind?'

He shook his head. 'It was Lizzie's idea.'

'Really?' I smiled. 'Lizzie's brilliant, isn't she, Dad?'

'*I* think so, yes.'

And it might have been my imagination, but I could almost swear Dad knew at that point that he definitely did want Lizzie to marry him.

Grandma phoned the following week and it turned out that she'd just heard back from Kirsten. Apparently Kirsten and Amanda's mother was still living at her last address, and she had passed Grandma's letter on to Kirsten, who had written answering Grandma's questions about the Mysterious Four Club.

'November the twenty-first was special because it was the date they started their club,' Grandma said. 'Remember I told you the first time we went to Brighton was in November, because it was my sister Esmerelda's birthday? Well, apparently that was when your mother first suggested they should start a secret club. I might have known it would be Claire's idea!'

'Will you bring Kirsten's letter with you when you come to see us, Grandma?' I asked excitedly.

'Of course, but Kirsten says you can also write to her yourself. I'm sure there's a lot more she can tell you about the Mysterious Four Club if you ask her.'

Dad and Lizzie were pleased when I told them my news, and even Matty was quite interested.

'It all makes perfect sense now, doesn't it?' Dad said.

I nodded. 'But there's another reason why November the twenty-first is so special,' I announced. 'It's *also* special because it's the date that Lizzie came all the way to Brighton to find me.'

'More fool her,' Matthew joked as he knelt down on the floor to tickle Hercule's tummy. 'Next time you should just leave her there, Lizzie.'

Lizzie put her arm round me protectively. 'I'm very glad I *did* find you, Esmie.'

'So am I,' I said happily. And it struck me that Lizzie had acted just like a mum that day, so in a way Nevada's prophecy had been right after all. I *had* met my mum at the end of the pier – not my birth mum, but my *new* mum.

'And you know what, Lizzie?' I added. 'If you and Dad *do* ever decide to get married, I honestly don't mind if it's in a registry office.'

'Just so long as they still need a bridesmaid, right, Esmie?' Matthew teased.

And to my amazement, instead of getting cross, Dad and Lizzie looked at each other and actually started to laugh.

A selected list of titles available from Macmillan Children's Books

The prices shown below are correct at the time of going to press. However, Macmillan Publishers reserves the right to show new retail prices on covers which may differ from those previously advertised.

Gwyneth Rees

The Mum Hunt	978-0-330-41012-0	£4.99
The Mum Detective	978-0-330-43453-9	£4.99
My Mum's from Planet Pluto	978-0-330-43728-8	£4.99
The Making of May	978-0-330-43732-5	£4.99

For younger readers

Mermaid Magic (3 books in 1)	978-0-330-42632-9	£4.99
Fairy Dust	978-0-330-41554-5	£4.99
Fairy Treasure	978-0-330-43730-1	£4.99
Fairy Dreams	978-0-330-43476-8	£4.99
Fairy Gold	978-0-330-43938-1	£4.99
Fairy Rescue	978-0-330-43971-8	£4.99
Cosmo and the Magic Sneeze	978-0-330-43729-5	£4.99
Cosmo and the Great Witch Escape	978-0-330-43733-2	£4.99

All Pan Macmillan titles can be ordered from our website, www.panmacmillan.com, or from your local bookshop and are also available by post from:

Bookpost, PO Box 29, Douglas, Isle of Man IM99 1BQ
Credit cards accepted. For details:
Telephone: 01624 677237
Fax: 01624 670923
Email: bookshop@enterprise.net
www.bookpost.co.uk

Free postage and packing in the United Kingdom